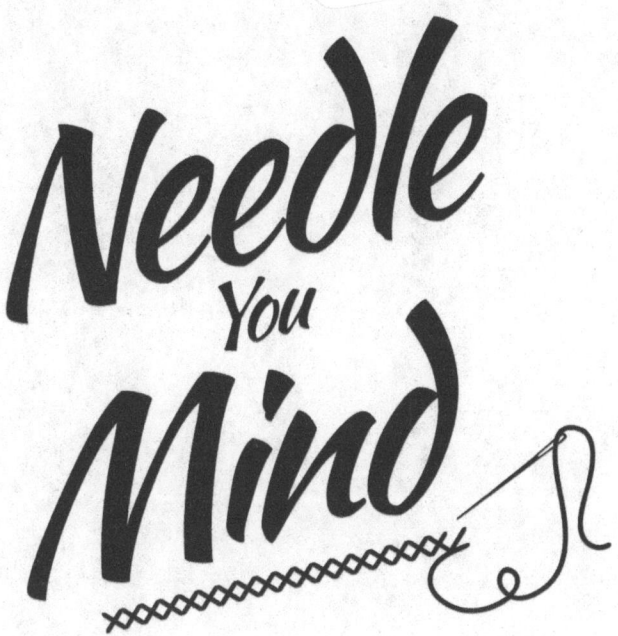

Needle You Mind

ACF Bookens

VINCI
BOOKS

By ACF Bookens

Vinci Books

vinci-books.com

Published by Vinci Books Ltd in 2025

1

Copyright © ACF Bookens 2023

A CIP catalogue record for this book is available from the British Library.

Paperback ISBN: 9781036704223

The EU GPSR authorised representative is Logos Europe, 9 rue Nicolas Poussion, 17000 La Rochelle, France

contact@logoseurope.eu

Chapter One

The tiny bunches of snowdrops planted in the unkept beds in front of the cottage were a true delight. Their dangling white heads made me think that pushing up through the partially frozen ground had been tiring, and the best they could do now was to dance in the wind with weariness.

They were a fitting match to the craftsman style of the house in one of the older neighborhoods of Octonia. I could almost picture the original owners stepping out on these first warm-ish days of spring and smiling at the bobbing flowers in their serpentine beds. Though now the old grass almost covered the flowers, the field stones that had once lined the winding beds were mostly buried in the soil. The house and garden had definitely seen better days.

But at least the new owners weren't tearing the house down. Sure, they were gutting it, and I imagined they had that modern white-gray, open-concept style that was the current trend in mind for the renovation. Still, the outside of the house, with its wide front porch and gabled windows, would keep its original flavor, and I was glad for that.

I was also grateful that the owners had allowed me to salvage some of the original details from the house. I had paid them a fair price for the chance to visit before they began demolition, and I was now ready to dig in.

It was a Friday afternoon, and Sawyer was with me. I hadn't taken him on salvage jobs before because, well, he had been a liability more than a help. But lately, he'd expressed interest in seeing what exactly I did in the "old buildings," as he called them, and if he was well-rested and well-fed, he could do a fair bit of work now that he was a bit older.

So I'd plied him with ice cream and promised him macaroni and cheese with broccoli, his new favorite combination, for dinner if he helped me get all the doorknobs off. He had been excited, and I had to admit, so was I.

When Sawyer's dad and I split, I wasn't sure how I would make ends meet, and it had been hard in the first months of this work. I'd had to get a lot of help and make some tough choices, choices that other people didn't like, about how to care for my child the best I could.

Things weren't exactly hunky-dory yet, but they were certainly better and easier. One of the things that had gotten much easier was that Sawyer was helpful in some of the best ways when he was fed and rested.

"Now, Saw, your job is to get the screws out of the doorknobs, okay?"

"Yep. Righty tighty, lefty loosey," Sawyer said in his still high-pitched voice. "You don't need to give me more constructions, Mama. I know what to do."

I smiled at my son's adorable malapropism and said, "Okay, no more instructions. Let's get to it."

Ignoring the lockbox, I let him do the honors of unlocking the front door and was delighted to see that almost everything was intact and that none of the wood-work had been painted. There was a fortune in wormy chestnut and maple finishes here, and my investment would pay for itself just in these two front rooms.

Right in the center of the front rooms, a hallway split the house going toward the back, and I could see it was lined with doors with crystal doorknobs.

"All right, Saw, I'm going to walk through the house while you get these doorknobs off. Let me know if you need help."

While I surreptitiously watched from the end of the hallway, he went to work on the first doorknob, slipping the first screw out of the door and into his pocket. He'd been sure to wear pants with pockets today.

Confident that he would make good progress or I'd hear the frustrated slam of a screwdriver against the floor if he didn't, I stepped into the kitchen, which mirrored the front two rooms of the house and was flanked by two entrances, one at each side of the room.

Directly in front of where I stood was a lovely dining room, with bright sunlight shining on a huge rectangular table from the massive windows beyond it. A hutch stood on the wall to my right, and to my left, the galley kitchen began with its black and white tile and stainless steel countertops. The space was lovely, and I could not imagine taking all this out in favor of marble and white cabinets—but it wasn't my house, and I was an "old soul," as my father always said.

I made my way around the corner to take a gander at the rest of the kitchen and poke at the tiles to see what I might be able to salvage, but as soon as I stepped into the full length of the space, I stopped cold.

In the middle of the floor was a woman—an unmoving woman. I rushed over to her and knelt to see if she was conscious. Her eyes were closed, and I couldn't see her chest rising with breath.

I slid my fingers against her throat, trying to do that thing people do in movies to see if someone was alive, but I couldn't tell if I was doing it right because I couldn't feel anything except the warmth of her body under my fingertips.

Just then, I heard the footfall of my little boy coming toward me, so I jumped up and intercepted him as he walked into the dining room, three crystal doorknobs in his hands. "Look what I got," he said with pure joy.

"Oh, that's great, Saw. Wow." I turned him back toward the hallway. "Show me where you got those."

We walked up the hall as Saw chattered about the doorknobs and showed me how he'd unscrewed each screw. Meanwhile, I quickly texted my husband, Santiago, the local sheriff. "Dead woman in the cottage. Come now. Sawyer is here."

His response was immediate. "Stay on the porch. You can't leave, but tell Saw I'm bringing him a surprise."

I slipped my phone back into my pocket and listened to my son prattle on about each turn of the screw. When he took a breath, I said, "Santiago is on his way with a surprise. Let's wait on the porch for him."

There was nothing that Sawyer loved more in the world than a surprise—well, except for maybe swimming. So it wasn't hard to steer him to the front door. "What kind of surprise is it?"

"If I told you, it wouldn't be a surprise, now would it?" I said as I tried to keep my tone light even as my heart pounded against my ribs.

"Can you give me a hint?" he said with a sly smile.

"I'm afraid not. He didn't tell me anything," I said

truthfully, even as I hoped that Santiago was actually bringing a surprise for the boy.

Not a minute later, Santiago's cruiser pulled up, and he jumped out with a huge blue balloon in hand. The passenger-side door swung open, and a tall, lean black man, Deputy Forest, my husband's newest hire, stepped out.

"Sawyer. Hey, bud," Santiago said as he ruffled the boy's hair and stepped onto the porch. "I need to ask your help. Do you have a minute?"

Sawyer looked up at me, and I nodded. "You've earned your wages for the day and are free to help another person in need," I said, still trying to keep the situation light until Sawyer was away from the crime scene.

"Okay, I can help," Sawyer said with a broad smile. "What do you need, Santi?"

"If it's okay with your mom, I need you to go with Deputy Forest and hang this balloon up at our house." Santiago's face was serious. "I want to try an experiment with it this afternoon, and I can't carry it around all day. Do you mind?"

Sawyer looked up at me again. "Mom, Santi needs me. Are you okay here by yourself?"

I nodded. "I am. Maybe Santiago can try his hand at doorknob removal?" I smiled at my husband.

"Be glad to," he said. "Laurent, you take my cruiser and assist Sawyer with this special duty, will you?"

Deputy Forest gave a crisp nod. "Glad to help the young lad," he said in a voice so deep that James Earl Jones would be jealous. "When we get to your house," he said as he turned to Sawyer, "you can do the siren and lights if you want."

Sawyer jumped over all the steps on the porch, trailing the giant balloon behind him. "I would love to," he said as the deputy opened the back door and held the balloon while Saw got himself strapped into the car seat that Santiago now kept there.

"See you later, love bug," I said as they pulled out. I waited until they turned the corner up the block before I fell against Santiago. "She was still warm," I said into his chest.

Santiago squeezed me quickly and then moved into the house. "And you're sure she is dead?"

A pang of panic went through my chest. "Oh no, maybe she's not. She was just so still, and it didn't look like she was breathing." I jogged to catch up to Santi. "What if she wasn't dead, and I didn't help her?"

Santiago led the way into the kitchen after I pointed out the doors at the end of the hall and then knelt where the woman was still prone on the black and white tile. He checked her pulse, just as I had, and shook his head. "No, she's definitely dead, and while not for long, I suspect she was dead when you found her."

He stood and looked at me. "You couldn't have saved her, Paisley." He took out his phone and called the coroner. "They'll be here in just a few minutes. Want to give me your statement on the porch?"

"Yes, please," I said as he took my hand and led me back outside. Sawyer and I had left our water bottles on the porch, and I picked mine up and took a long swig. Then I told my husband what had happened.

"That's it. You walked in, saw her, checked for a pulse, then texted me?" He looked at me carefully. "Did you notice anything else?"

I drew a very long breath and closed my eyes, trying to do what I knew he needed me to do—notice details.

I went through my thought process as we came into the house—the woodwork, the beautiful table, the— "Yes, there was a glass on the dining room table." I opened my eyes. "Was it there just now?"

Santiago shook his head. "No. No, it was not. The table was clear. I noticed that specifically."

A lump the size of a grapefruit formed in my throat. "Someone moved it then while I was here. While Sawyer was here."

Chapter Two

The forensics team, a new addition to Octonia's law enforcement contingent, arrived quickly with the coroner's van behind. Within an hour, they had dusted the scene for prints, taken photographs, and loaded up the woman's body for an autopsy.

During that time, news had spread that I had found another body. Unfortunately, I had gained a reputation for being the first on the scene of several murders. While that reputation hadn't turned into suspicion of me thus far, I was still beginning to feel very self-conscious that I kept finding these bodies.

That unease arose when my best friend Mika showed up just as the coroner left and said, "The reporter from the Charlottesville news station just came by my shop looking for you."

The blood drained from my upper body. "What did you tell him?"

"That we'd had a huge fight, and you had been banned

from my shop." She grinned. "I figured that would give us one place he couldn't find you."

I sighed. "Good thinking. I'll have to get Saul to lock up the construction yard for a bit."

"I don't know about all that," Saul said as he came onto the cottage's porch and stood beside me. "I put a couple of guys near your store and instructed them to keep anyone snooping away from you and your shop."

"I'm so sorry," I said. "I thought all this would have died down by now." I leaned against the porch railing. "You'd think people would have other things to do rather than be that interested in what one single mom does."

"You are overestimating the amount of interesting things in Octonia, dear girl," Saul said. "Besides, you are pretty interesting."

I sighed again. A few weeks earlier, a local reporter had done a story on me, ostensibly to highlight my business and work in architectural salvage. Instead, he'd spun the story to make it about the murders I'd helped to solve in the past few years. He'd gone so far as to suggest, carefully to avoid libel, that I might have been at least pleased with my discoveries if not outright involved in the deaths that created all those bodies.

The newspaper article had created a maelstrom of controversy in our small town. Most of the people of Octonia had rallied to my defense and taken on the "outsider" who dared malign one of their own. But, unfortunately, one of the board of supervisors had seized upon the opportunity to try to increase her chances of winning the next election and had asked Sheriff Shifflett, a man she somehow didn't know was my husband, to investigate me.

He had outright refused, and she had threatened him, a fact that became front-page news itself. For weeks, Santi and

I were the talk of the town. It had even gotten so bad that Sawyer had come home one day and asked if murder was good for business, a phrase he'd heard one of his teachers use.

We'd downplayed that comment as being silly and had, thus far, kept Sawyer out of most of the fray around these rumors, but this new body, and his presence when I found it, was going to make things so much harder to keep from him.

Not to mention that this could affect my business. Just thinking through all that so soon after the shock of finding that woman on the floor left me so weak I could hardly stand. So I decided not to and let my body slide to the porch floor, my water bottle grasped between my knees.

"I don't know how much more of this I can take," I said as I put my forehead on the top of the bottle. "Maybe I need to find another line of work."

Mika slid down to sit next to me. "Absolutely not. You are so good at this work, Paisley. People love what you do and your stories about what you find. You cannot quit." She smiled at me with a gleam of mischief that I could see even from the corner of my eye. "We need to get in front of this story."

I heard what she said, but it took me a minute to process it. When I finally looked up at her, she had that little furrow between her brows that meant she was scheming. "What do you mean? Mika, no shenanigans."

"Never," she said with more force than necessary. "All I mean is that you should solve this murder and write about it in your newsletter before anyone else can. Show that you're aware of your penchant for finding dead people and that you are as committed to solving these crimes as anyone."

"What's this about solving crimes?" Santiago asked as

he sat down on the other side of me. "You two aren't planning anything, are you?"

"No," I said. "Mika just has some loony idea that I could solve this murder and write about the case before the news can get hold of it."

"Um," Santi said as he stood up. "I think it may be too late for that." He looked over the railing to where the local news truck was setting up across the street. "Slip out the alleyway. I'll get your car and bring it around," he said as he straightened his hat and walked up the sidewalk to meet the quickly approaching reporter.

I didn't hesitate and quickly went down the front steps, around the side, and up the alley toward the back. I was tempted to pull my shirt over my head just like the people do outside courthouses when they don't want to be photographed, but I figured that might just draw more, not less, attention to me.

A few moments later, Santiago drove my Subaru up the small alley behind the house, and I got into the passenger seat. "How did you get rid of him?"

"I threatened to have harassment charges brought against him if I saw him within a hundred feet of you." Santi smiled. "That seemed to work."

I groaned. "This is awful." I put my hands over my face. "But not as bad as it was for that poor woman. Do we know who she was? I don't think I've ever seen her before."

Santi shook his head. "No idea. We didn't find a purse or ID or anything, so she's a Jane Doe until we can identify her."

"I expect you're already doing this, but did you talk to the owners of the house?"

He smiled and patted my hand on my leg. "Yes, we will do that. You have their contact info, right?"

"I do," I said. "Maybe I should tell them." I really didn't want to do that, but I'd never been good at determining what was a real responsibility of mine and what I just felt like I should do because I felt responsible for everything.

"No, love. I'll tell them, and we'll figure out the next steps for your salvage job together, okay?"

For a few moments, I just let my nervous system settle, but then a thought occurred to me. "What was with the balloon?"

Santi huffed out a quick chuckle. "It was the best surprise I could think of at the moment. The dispatcher's birthday was today, and she'd had a delivery. Was happy for me to take the balloon off her hands."

"Smart thinking," I said. "What did you tell Forest to do with it?"

"Hang it on the porch and tell Saw it was a weather balloon."

I looked over at my husband. "A weather balloon?"

"Well, he'll at least be able to tell if it's windy."

I sighed out a laugh and put my head back on the seat.

When we got home, I was relieved to find that I could sit back entirely while Santi did all the work. The owners of the house, Mr. and Mrs. Cubbins, identified the dead woman as Viola McNamara, the daughter of the people they had bought the house from. Deputy Forest had gone by their house as soon as my dad had come to stay with Saw, and they'd immediately recognized Ms. McNamara from the photo he showed them.

Dad took Sawyer to my ex-husband's house as soon as we arrived home and got to wish the boy a good weekend, and then, I was deep into land record research to recover the chain of title for the cottage. Within a few minutes, and with a little help from the county clerk's office staff, I found that the house had only had two owners—the McNamaras, who had built the house in 1919, and the Cubbins themselves.

I showed my brief notes to Santiago and said, "Not much to uncover here. But in the house itself. . ." I let my sentence trail off, hoping I wouldn't have to directly ask for what I was hinting at.

Fortunately, my husband knew me well, and he nodded. "The scene is already cleared, and the Cubbins are fine with you resuming work, with police presence, of course."

"As long as that presence is you, I don't mind at all." I leaned over and kissed his cheek. "But they don't have any idea why she was in the house? She hadn't asked to do a last visit or anything?"

"No, according to Forest, they would have been fine with her visiting, but she never asked. They'd met her at the closing when they purchased the house but hadn't had any other contact."

I stood up, got us a wine glass each, and poured sparkling cider before sitting back down. "Maybe she just thought she was entitled to go in, especially if she grew up there." I shook my head. "Could it have been she didn't think she was trespassing?"

"Beats me," Santi said. "People are weird"—he winked—"as we know. Maybe?"

"But then that begs the question—why did someone kill her there?" I stared at my almost blank page of notes. "You don't think the Cubbins are hiding something, do you?"

Santi huffed out a sigh. "Maybe. I'll definitely talk to them again and see if they can shed any light on the situation." He tapped the table with one finger. "But what do you say we do some on-site investigation tomorrow?"

I smiled. "Does that mean you'll help me pull things out of the house, too?"

"Now, I didn't say that," he teased with another wink. "Of course. Let's start early, though. I'm kind of wanting to grill out and watch a movie tomorrow night."

"Perfect," I said as I looked at my nearly blank sheet of paper. "At the very least, we'll know the house well by the end of the day."

"By which you mean, we'll be covered in sawdust and spider webs, correct?" he said with a laugh. "I can't wait."

At six the next morning, we were in the cottage driveway with two giant coffees and two even more enormous apple fritters in hand. It was still dark outside, and we'd had a light frost overnight, which meant I was giddy. I loved chilly mornings, a fact my husband thought ridiculous as he sat shivering next to me, even with the seat heater on high. "Are you ready?" I said with my knees bouncing up and down in excitement.

"I would have been more ready at nine after two cups of coffee and another of these fritters, but I was a scout, so you know . . ."

"Always prepared," I said. "Race you to the door." I charged up the driveway and onto the steps, where I immediately lost my footing on the frost-covered wood and tumbled into the banister, spilling my coffee and nearly losing my fritter.

Santi rushed up to steady me, and I leaned against him

as I laughed at myself. "You didn't marry me for my grace, that's for sure," I said.

"You have many other redeeming qualities," he said, taking the keys from my hand and unlocking the cottage door.

My laughter stopped immediately. I had tried to convince myself that I had seen enough dead bodies by now not to be affected deeply by seeing another one, but clearly, that was not the case. As soon as I stepped inside the door, my heart started to race, and it took a sheer force of effort for me to walk back and look into the kitchen again.

Of course, it was empty, and if there had been any signs of death from Ms. McNamara's body, the crime scene team had cleaned them up thoroughly. I let out a long, slow breath as I set my fritter and now half-empty coffee cup on the dining room table behind me.

"I suppose you don't know how she died," I said as Santiago pulled out a chair, and we both sat down.

He tilted his head and looked at me. "Even in a major metro area, Paisley, it would take a couple of days to get autopsy results. We live in Octonia. And it's Saturday."

"Fair enough," I said. "Okay, let's get to work."

Santiago shoved half his fritter into his mouth and mumbled something that sounded like, "Whef tog, bo?"

I laughed. "Let's start at the front with the mantels. Saul should be here soon with a truck to haul stuff to the shop."

Just as we walked into the front rooms, I heard the unmistakable sound of a big truck backing up and saw a massive moving truck edging toward the front steps.

"Wow, he's expecting a big load," Santiago said as he joined me at the window.

"I did tell him most of the paneling was in great shape," I said quietly.

"Guess I won't have to go to the gym this weekend then," he said with a smile. "And we do have Epsom salts at home."

"And a bathtub big enough for two," I said with a wink before I turned and opened the door to welcome Saul and Mika.

"Brought along some muscle," Saul said.

My best friend and Saul's niece raised her right arm and flexed her tiny bicep. "Just point me at the stuff that needs demolishing."

"All right there, muscles. Slow your roll. We're delicately removing things, not demolishing."

Mika pouted. "So no sledgehammer?"

"I'll let you at a wall when we get the good stuff out. How's that?"

Her face lit up, as did mine, when she handed me a coffee bigger than I'd brought. "Thank you," I said.

"And one for you, sir," Saul said to Santiago as he handed Santiago an equally large cup. "We starting up here?"

"We are," I said. "If possible, I'd like to get this paneling and the mantels as well as these pillars and bookshelves."

Mika groaned. "So basically everything in the room?"

"Yep," I said. I was already thinking about how to stage this as a room for a potential buyer. If someone really wanted that authentic craftsman feel in their living space, these pieces would do just that, no matter what age the building. "You two want to start over there." I pointed to the right, where the mantel looked a little easier to remove.

"Sounds good," Saul said and headed toward the mantel with a very menacing-looking crowbar. I braced myself for the sound of splintering wood, but I was pleasantly surprised to hear only the scratching of nails pulling loose instead.

Santi applied gentle pressure to the side of the mantel in front of us, and soon enough, both pieces were out, wrapped in blankets, and in the truck. The paneling continued in the same fashion, except for one corner piece that splintered as Mika pulled it free—a minor loss in an otherwise successful venture.

Soon enough, we had stripped the room bare except for the floorboards, which we decided to wait on while we loaded everything else. After all, it wasn't the wisest move to carry sinks and such across bare floor joists.

While Saul and Mika tackled the built-ins and bathroom fixtures in the rooms along the hallway, Santi and I headed back to the kitchen. "You sure you don't want them to do this room? Save yourself the flashbacks?"

I shook my head. "The only way out is through, and I think I can better purge the images of Ms. McNamara's body by working in the space. It'll look very different when we're done."

We began in the kitchen proper. The cabinets were vintage and still sported the original butter-yellow color, but I knew from experience that the wood was probably quite dry. Sure enough, as soon as we started to separate them from the wall, they began to split apart. So we left those and focused on the tiles.

Tiles like these, originals from the early twentieth century, could fetch a dollar, sometimes two, in my shop, so I hoped we'd be able to remove a bunch of them. Santiago started at the other end of the kitchen floor by the back door, and I took my mini crowbar to the backsplash. The tiles popped loose easily, and I was soon trucking along at a good pace, removing tiles and then stacking them on the counter to be boxed up.

Santiago was having a bit more trouble with the floor tiles, but by the time I got to the sink about halfway across the room, he was cruising back toward me a row at a time. In fact, I was enjoying his process of shimmying his hips while he worked the pry bar under a tile that I almost plunged my tool right through the plasterboard above the sink.

"Gracious," I shouted as I pulled my pry bar loose and watched the tile it had been behind shatter in the ceramic sink below. "Darn."

"We have a few others, Pais," Santiago said as he wrestled another complete tile free.

"I know. I just think that every single one of these is funding Sawyer's college education."

"I really don't think we need to worry about that just yet," he said.

"It'll be here sooner than I think, or at least that's what all the moms on Facebook say." I chuckled and turned back to remove another tile.

As I popped it off the wall, I noticed a dark patch in the plaster. "Looks like there might have been a leak here. I'll make a note to tell the Cubbins."

But as the next tile came loose, I saw it wasn't a dark patch but a hole. "Whoa," I said.

"What?" Santi said as he stepped closer. "Oh, yeah, whoa." He leaned in. "Is there something in there?"

I wedged my belly against the sink and leaned forward so far that my feet came off the floor. Sure enough, there was a small gold-colored box with an envelope beneath it tucked into the hole. I pulled them out gently, unsure how old the items were and not wanting to destroy them with a rough grab.

The box was about the size of my palm and textured as if it had been covered in fancy, gold wrapping paper. The top lifted off easily, and a bejeweled gold broach was shaped like a Christmas tree. "Wow," I said, lifting it out of the box. "It's heavy."

"And tacky," Santi said. "Very tacky."

"You're not wrong," I said, but it must have been special if someone hid it away like that. I studied the pin for another minute. "Why would someone hide this away so completely? That's weird."

"What's in the envelope?" Santi asked.

I handed him the small white packet, and he pulled out a pink piece of paper folded precisely in thirds vertically. "To Viola, my love. For when you need to remember me. Always, Abe," he read.

I carried the box over to the countertop with Santi close behind. "A secret love affair," I said.

"Seems that Ms. McNamara had some stories to tell," he said as he carefully slid the note back into the envelope.

I studied the Christmas tree closely and turned it over. "It's signed." I stood up and walked over to the light. "Cartier."

"Holy cow," he said. "Did you say Cartier?"

"I most certainly did," I replied as I dug my phone out of my back pocket and googled Cartier Christmas tree. Sure enough, the pin popped right up, and it was worth almost $25,000. I turned the phone to Santi, and we stared dumbly at the pin for a few moments as the magnitude of what we'd found sunk in.

"I have to tell the Cubbins," I said.

"You do. And I think we may now know why she was here."

"You think she came back for the pin?" I asked. "She must have known it was valuable."

Santi looked at the image on my phone screen again. "Maybe. But I'm wondering if it was more the sentiment she wanted to recall."

"Hmm. I can't remember if she was married or not. I'm guessing not since she kept her maiden name, but I need to look into that." I opened my genealogy app and started to search.

Santi put a hand over my phone screen. "Let's finish up with the salvage work first. We have help now."

I sighed and clicked off my phone. "You're right. I'll find out more later."

By the time we finished salvaging everything, including the floors from the front rooms, it was almost three in the afternoon. We hadn't stopped to eat, and all of us were starving. Santi invited Saul and Mika over for dinner and said they should feel free to bring anyone they'd like.

Then, as he and Saul went to unload the truck, Mika and I took my car to the grocery store to get hamburgers, hot dogs, and deli salads for dinner. Santi wanted to grill, but we didn't need to make this an elaborate meal.

Soon, Mika and I were headed to my house with dinner and dessert—a banana cream pie from the freezer section—and when the guys arrived a bit later, we had everything ready for the grill and cocktails.

It was a cool evening, so while Santi grilled on the front

porch, Saul and I started a fire in the fire pit and got it good and warm. Mika poured us all Bailey's and coffee, and when her boyfriend Dom arrived, we were just ready to eat.

We'd already told Saul and Mika about the broach and the note, but I didn't mind telling Dom about it again. "So you think she came back to get the pin, and that's when someone killed her?" he said. "Do you think they knew about the broach?"

I sat back in my camp chair and stared at him. "Maybe they killed her for it," I said as the thought occurred to me for the first time.

"Yeah, I wondered the same thing," Santi said as he set the plate of burgers and dogs on the folding table we'd set up by the fire. "But if they knew something was valuable there, wouldn't they have looked for it? It didn't seem like the house had been disturbed at all."

Saul nodded as he put an impressive amount of mayo and lettuce on his burger. "But maybe they just went through drawers and things. There weren't many, and they could have been careful."

"Right," Mika added. "No one was living there, so they had all the time in the world to look through things and then put them back."

I thought about how the house had looked when Sawyer and I had gone in for the first time yesterday. The place hadn't felt empty, somehow, but I had chalked that up to the fact that it was clean, with no dust in sight. Now, though, that tidiness seemed a tad bit too conspicuous.

"They cleaned up after themselves," I said.

"In more ways than one, it seems," Dom said.

"Poor Ms. McNamara," Mika said. "She probably didn't know they were watching the house."

"Or maybe they were watching her," Santi said.

Suddenly, what had simply been an odd, mysterious event felt much more sinister.

Chapter Three

One of the things you learn when you do historical research about every day people is that we really are a culture only interested in the sensational and extraordinary. Even our "Everyday Heroes" are people who do incredibly selfless things, things so generous and amazing that they stand out.

But you don't usually make the news when you're just a regular person who does their job, takes care of their family, and has a few friends. It turned out that Viola McNamara was a pretty ordinary person.

I tried to remember that probably meant she had a good, simple life, but her quiet existence made things anything but simple to me. I couldn't find anything about her online—no birth certificate, no marriage certificate, and no mentions in the local newspaper. I even tried asking about her at church that Sunday morning, but no one at Bethel had heard of her.

"Oh her," one older woman finally said when I described Ms. McNamara's old house. "She was sweet."

"Sweet." It was not exactly a firestorm of information.

At lunch with my friend Mary and some of the folks from church, Santi and I told them about Ms. McNamara's death since that was already common knowledge, seeing as how any excitement spread as if we had a town crier on the corner of Main Street.

But Santi didn't want to reveal that we'd found the note and the broach, mostly because this was an active murder investigation but also because of the value of that Christmas tree. Making some unusual and illegal choices was easy when twenty-five grand was involved.

On the way over, he'd said, "We don't need anyone else to come and look for that pin."

I was dying to tell Mary. She was one of my closest friends, and I really wanted to talk to her about Abe and Viola. But I had to respect Santi's wishes, both maritally and professionally. He was the sheriff, after all.

"So, do you know how she died?" Mary asked after I finished telling the group about how I'd found the body.

Santi sighed loudly. "I need just one TV drama to show that coroners take weekends. Just one."

"The autopsy won't be performed until Monday," I said by way of clarification. "But from what I saw when I checked to see if she was breathing, there wasn't any blood."

"So she probably wasn't shot or hit with a blunt object," said a tiny woman who sang soprano in the church choir.

"Were her eyes bloodshot? Did you notice any marks on her neck?" the church custodian asked.

Santi groaned. "Seriously, folks, stop watching crime shows. Let the coroner do his job."

I patted his knee. "From what I've heard, this new guy is really good at his job. I'm sure we'll know more when it can be shared." Even when Santi got the results, I would be lucky if he told me, his wife. The cause of death wasn't something he was likely to write a press release about.

Just then, his phone rang. "Well, look at that. Speak of the devil," he said as he got up and went out to Mary's front porch.

"Well, isn't that some timing?" Mary said. She stood up and peeked through the curtains, lingering a bit longer than necessary.

"Mary," I scolded. "Give the man some privacy."

"What?" she said as she threw her hands up in the air. "The curtains were a bit dusty. Just cleaning them is all."

Now, it was time for me to groan. "Just do Santi a favor. If you hear anything," I said to everyone in the room, "please make him your first call."

All the heads in the room bobbed in agreement. "Absolutely," the soprano said. "That sweet woman deserves justice."

Again, everyone nodded, and soon after, Santi returned and said he needed to go. "I can drop you home if you'd like."

"Yeah, that would be good," I said. "Thank you, everyone." I went to the dining room and retrieved my casserole dish that was, I was pleased to see, completely cleaned out of green bean casserole. It looked like the homemade onion strings had been a hit.

Santi was quiet, as he usually was when he was letting new information sift into place in his brain. When we pulled into the driveway, I leaned over and kissed him. "Too bad the new coroner works on weekends after all."

He gave me a small smile. "I may be late. Read Saw our book for me, will you?"

"Of course," I said. "Be safe."

He nodded, then pulled back out of the driveway.

I went inside and spent the next hour or so getting the house ready for bed, a process which included laying our copy of *Percy Jackson* on Sawyer's bed so that I wouldn't forget to read him a chapter like Santi did every night.

Soon after, Saw's dad dropped him off, and the boy looked like he might drop from fatigue. "Looks like you had a good time?" I said.

"Too much fun," he said. "When is it night time?"

"Soon, love bug. Why don't you go watch some videos, and we'll go up in a bit." It was only 5:30, but when my little boy wanted to go to bed, I knew he needed to go to bed.

By seven, he was snoozing away in his racecar bed, and I was settled at the small desk I'd tucked into the corner of my bedroom, my laptop open. I knew I could find something about Viola McNamara if I just looked hard enough.

Unfortunately, all my usual genealogical and historical resources continued to come up short. Viola just wasn't on any public records except the title for her home, and since she'd inherited that and then sold it only recently, she basically had a public record of two mentions.

I was getting pretty frustrated when I decided to try good, old Google. I typed in "Viola McNamara and Abe" on a whim and was delighted when an engagement announcement in the local paper popped up. "Abraham Tuskins and Viola McNamara have announced their intention to be married on August 23 at St. Paul's Methodist Church in Octonia." The article continued with a brief background on Abe and Viola, both graduates of Octonia High. Abe was attending the University of Virginia, and Viola had just finished a secretarial certificate. According to the article, the two would be living on Maple Street in downtown Octonia, number 318.

Once I got over my surprise that the newspaper would print people's home addresses for all to see, I made notes. So Abe was Viola's fiancé. His name was Abraham Tuskins, and a quick search brought up a fair number of records about him, including a listing as a professor emeritus of psychology at the University of Virginia, his alma mater.

A quick search of the local GIS records for the surrounding counties gave me his address, just east of Octonia in Barbourton. While it was possible he had died and the property was still in his name, it was far more likely he was still alive and living just twenty minutes away.

I continued finding out more about Mr. Tuskins, who had lived quite a distinguished life with numerous articles published in premier law journals, several awards from both the University and other organizations, and what it seemed was a very successful and well-praised law practice. He wasn't famous or even a person that people in his neighborhood would probably have known for his work, but he was well-renowned in his field.

I was just writing down some final thoughts about Abe and a list of questions about Viola when Santiago got home. I heard him downstairs, quietly moving through the house in a routine that was now so familiar I could trace it in my mind. He stopped in the kitchen for his glass of ice water. Then he hung up his holster and took off his shoes on the hall tree at the bottom of the stairs before coming up, kissing me on the cheek, and immediately locking his pistol in the gun safe at the back of our closet.

While he was getting into bed, I heard the soft pitter-pat of furry feet and got out of my desk chair just in time for my cat, Beauregard, to take the seat. I had learned the hard way that if Beau didn't get to sleep where he wanted, I would feel the wrath of his claws on my leg while he pitty-patted me into submission. I was a fast learner.

I got into bed next to Santi and turned toward him. "You okay?"

He nodded. "Yeah, but this case. . . I can't say more, but it's, well, a lot."

My husband was not easily overwhelmed, but I could see from the clench in his jaw that he was feeling the pressure on this one. And I knew why. He'd been re-elected the previous year by a thin margin, thanks in large part to a racist campaign strategy by his opponent, and now every significant crime in Octonia gave those who critiqued him fodder for their fire. Santi wanted to have this job until he retired because he loved it and Octonia, so he was always determined to do his best work.

This level of pressure was more than usual, though, and if he couldn't talk about it, then it was much more than usual. Santi was always thoughtful about what he shared with me, careful to keep his professional ethics in line. But he also often used me as a sounding board, a safe place to work out his thoughts without undermining his leadership or authority.

If he wasn't telling me something, it was because he absolutely could not. However, I had no ethical obligation to keep what I had discovered a secret, so while we settled in for the night, I went over what I had found out about Viola and Abe's engagement and about Tuskins himself. "I'm thinking you might want to talk to him."

Santi nodded. "I do, but I can't just yet." He reached over and took my hand. "You, however, can certainly reach out. Maybe for one of your newsletter articles?"

I half sat up in bed. "Are you actually asking me to butt into one of your investigations?" I pretended to be shocked because most people reacted like I was intruding when I helped with a case. But the truth of the matter was that Santi and I had built our relationship around solving these murders I kept stumbling upon. It was just part of how we operated. I wasn't a busybody, and he wasn't incompetent. We were just a good team.

"Stop it," he said with a quiet laugh. "Seriously, though, would you go interview him, see if he knows anything that might be useful?"

I kissed him lightly. "Of course. I'll head over as soon as I get Saw to school. Should have a report for you by lunch."

He smiled. "Thank you. You are the best."

I went to sleep content but worried. What exactly was going on with Viola McNamara's case to make my stalwart husband so concerned?

The next morning, Sawyer was bouncing with excitement about going to school because it was his week to take care of the class turtle. I'd tried to understand why feeding a turtle exactly two slices of apple and two pieces of spinach a day was so fun, but I had to admit my imagination simply did not extend that far.

The upside of this situation was that my little man did not stall even a little bit about going to school, so we were through the drop-off line in record time. Which meant I reached Barbouton at 8:20 a.m. I had decided against calling ahead to Judge Tuskins because I had learned from my husband that it was often best not to give someone time to think ahead when discussing a murder. Even if they weren't guilty, most people got defensive and anxious in light of someone's untimely death.

Still, I wasn't cruel, and this man was retired. I decided I couldn't arrive at his house before nine in the morning, so I pulled into a cute little coffee shop on the town's Main Street and chuckled at its name, Brew-Ti-Full. Inside, the space was cozy and clean and smelled like freshly baked cookies, and when the woman at the counter made me a delicious vanilla latte and plated a cinnamon chip scone that was so warm I could see the steam coming off of it, I decided I might have to come to Barbourton more often.

I sat at a table by the window and took out my laptop so I could spend a bit of time updating my inventory and checking my sales figures. Lately, I'd been foregoing the auction sites and relying on my own marketing to bring people to my online store. It had been a bit of a slow start, but folks were learning to come to me for the rarer salvage items, like radiators with original paint or large stained glass windows.

Today, I was pleased to see that the weekend had brought about a number of big sales, including an antique pie safe that I had rescued from my very first paid salvage gig. The buyers had even sprung for express shipping, so I was pleased to find out that my assistant, Claire, had already been in touch with the shipping company and that they were coming out that afternoon to box up the piece and get it on the road.

My pleasure must have shown on my face because a man sitting at the table next to me caught my eye as he got up to go to the counter for a refill. "Good news, I take it," he said with a wide smile that revealed perfect, white teeth.

"Oh yes, just a good day for my business. Thanks," I said as I returned his grin. "You're just lucky I didn't let out a woo-hoo."

He laughed. "Oh, joy is not something I ever want to

miss out on. Glad things are going well. Do you mind if I ask what your business is?" He set his empty cup down and stood by my table.

"Oh, I'm in architectural salvage. It's really fun."

"I bet," he said and pulled out the chair across from me. "Do you mind?"

I was not the most extroverted person, but this man with thinning gray hair and a finely pressed polo shirt seemed kind enough. And, as Mika was always telling me, I had to learn to network more and share my enthusiasm for what I do. "You never know who might be a potential customer," she had said so many times that I could hear her voice in my head.

"Sure, please." I put out my hand. "I'm Paisley Sutton."

"Abraham Tuskins," he said as he took my fingers in his.

If I hadn't been sitting down, I probably would have lost my balance and fallen over with shock. "Nice to meet you, Mr. Tuskins," I said.

My brain was whirring as I tried to decide if I should tell him I was on my way to see him or just find a way to work the conversation around to Viola when he decided for me.

"Oh, you're over in Octonia, aren't you? I've been by your shop. You have lovely things." His smile was still big and genuine.

"Why, thank you," I said as I decided to let the conversation flow naturally. "Are you interested in history?"

He shook his head. "Not particularly. I'm more into the world of the mind, but Octonia is where I grew up. And your shop seemed like the kind of place that would bring back some good memories."

I was a terrible liar, so I didn't even try to fib my way

around the fact that I already knew he was from Octonia. "You haven't thought of moving back?"

At this question, his smile fell. "No, I'm afraid there are some not-so-good memories there, too. It's enough for me to visit."

Even though I felt bad that Mr. Tuskins was clearly saddened by the past, I wasn't about to let that stop me from achieving the purpose of my visit. "I do understand that. My job brings me into contact with a strange number of sad events. Just last week, in fact, I found the body of a woman who had been murdered in the house I was salvaging from."

"Oh my," he said. "That must have been a shock. Are you okay?" I could almost see him evaluating my story. "Have you talked to anyone about it?"

"I have, thank you. I'm married to the sheriff, and he and I are both pretty good about being open about this kind of thing. Part of the deal, I guess." I didn't know why I was telling this stranger personal details about me, but when I took a breath and paused, I found I didn't mind sharing with him. That was probably a trick of his trade.

"So, at the risk of being nonchalant but also wanting to respect what I expect is an active police investigation, were you able to complete your salvage work in the house?" Mr. Tuskins' question was so courteous that I didn't hesitate to answer.

"We were, fortunately. It was a classic craftsman cottage, but the new owners didn't want all the original wood. So we got some columns, a couple of mantels, this beautiful wood floor, and a beautiful collection of black and white tile from the kitchen." I was about to tell him about the doorknobs and how Sawyer had such joy getting them, but then I noticed that all the color had gone out of his face.

"You were the one who found Viola's body?" He rasped.

I took a deep breath. "You knew Ms. McNanamara."

He nodded very slowly. "At one time, we were engaged to be married."

I didn't want to deceive this kind man, so I didn't even try to feign surprise. "Oh my. I'm so sorry for your loss." I reached over and put my hand over his. "Did you stay in touch?"

He shook his head. "No, once the marriage was off, I thought it best to keep my distance. For both of us." He sighed heavily. "Do they know how she died?"

I shook my head. "How did you hear about her death?"

"Her niece, Olivia, called me. She's Viola's only living relative, and I guess she figured I'd like to know."

The color still had not returned to his face, and I was a bit worried about the older man. "I suppose that means Viola must have spoken of you fondly," I said, hoping that might give him a bit of comfort.

He smiled wanly. "I hope that is what that means. After all, we loved each other deeply."

I literally bit my tongue to keep myself from asking why they hadn't married then. That felt just too invasive. Instead, I just sat silently.

After a few moments, he sat up a bit straighter. "She was a lovely woman. And I'm so sorry you had to find her like that." He leaned in. "I trust your husband will do his very best to find out who did this to Viola."

"He absolutely will," I said and noticed his mouth tightened just a little at that statement. "He's very good at his job."

"I'm sure he is, dear. You don't stay in a position like that unless you know what you're doing." At that, he slid his chair back and stood. "I've taken enough of your time, Ms. Sutton. Thank you."

I reached into my bag and pulled out my card. "Please, if you want to see some of the things we salvaged from Ms. McNamara's house, give me a call. It's not much, but if it would give you some comfort. . ."

"Thank you, dear," he said. "You're very kind." With that, he turned and walked out of the store, his empty coffee cup still on my table.

Chapter Four

I immediately texted Santi about the fortuitous encounter with Judge Tuskins and told him something had intervened with Judge Tuskins' and Viola's marriage plans. "I'm not sure how to look into that, but I'm going to start with her niece, Olivia," I told him.

The next text from my husband was a phone number for Olivia Weiss. What a good man.

I hated when people had phone conversations in coffee shops, even as I knew they were sometimes unavoidable, so I returned to my car with a refill of coffee and two of those scones for home.

Olivia Weiss answered with a joyful "Halloo!"

"Hello, Ms. Weiss?"

"Yes, this is Olivia. To whom do I have the pleasure of speaking?"

I smiled. This woman was not only pleasant but had perfect grammar. Those were both good things in my mind. "This is Paisley Sutton. I'm sorry to call at such a sad time."

"Oh yes, Ms. Sutton. You discovered Aunt Viola's body. Thank you for making sure she was cared for."

I couldn't imagine what kind of person would have done anything differently than I did, but I simply said, "Of course," and then delved on. "I was speaking with Abraham Tuskins this morning, and he mentioned that you had called him to inform him of your aunt's death."

"Oh yes. Poor man. He was so torn up, but I knew he would want to know. He was the love of Aunt Viola's life."

"He said much the same thing when we were talking, but, and forgive me for being so direct, if they loved each other so much, why did they not marry?"

I could hear Olivia take a deep breath on the other end of the line. "It's a true tragedy, one of those horrific moments where prejudice did its worst." She sighed again. "You see, Judge Tuskins is Jewish."

The silence stretched between us while I tried to figure out what the man's ethnic heritage had to do with this conversation, but then it clicked. "Her family wouldn't allow her to marry him?"

"And his wouldn't allow him to marry her. From what Aunt Viola said, it was really ugly, and eventually, they couldn't fight their families and called the engagement off." The happiness in her voice was totally gone now. "It was the saddest event of my aunt's entire life, and honestly, I don't think she ever recovered."

I swallowed hard to clear the tears from my throat. "That is absolutely heartbreaking, even from decades later."

"Absolutely. You know, she never married," Olivia continued. "It was a profound tragedy."

"It sounds like it. Do you know how they met?"

A bit of laughter came back into Olivia's voice. "Now,

that is a great story. Would you like to grab an early lunch so I can share it in person?"

I looked at my watch—just 10:30—but if the niece of a murdered woman wanted to meet, I wasn't going to say no. "Sounds great. Where do you live?" Her area code covered most of the surrounding counties, so it didn't give me any clue.

"Tiny place called Reva, but there's no place to eat here. Want to meet in Madison at that farm-to-table place? You know it?"

I smiled. "I do, and that sounds great. I can eat their pimento cheese burger any time of day."

"Same," Olivia said. "See you in thirty?"

"Perfect," I said. That would give me just enough time to drive over after filling Santi in on this new development. I thought he would be pleased.

Santi was pleased but also a bit concerned that this guy, whom I had been going to surprise with a visit, surprised me instead. "You didn't tell anyone else what you were doing?"

"Not even Mika," I said. "You were the only one who knew. Did you tell anyone?"

"Not even Forest," he said. There was silence on the line for a long moment, and then he said, "I suppose it was a coincidence, but I still don't like it."

I laughed. "I hear you, and we were in public. I was completely safe."

"I know. You're a wise woman, Paisley Sutton. It's just part of my makeup to question things."

"And that's part of why I love you. Curiosity is very sexy, you know?" I said.

He hung up, laughing, as I pulled into the parking lot behind Mad Local. I had been to this restaurant several times, and I still couldn't quite figure out what the original purpose of the building had been. A mechanic's garage? A storefront? I just wasn't sure, but I loved it. I had even briefly toyed with putting my salvage shop in the adjacent space. Quickly, though, it became clear I'd need more space and could use the free space that Saul had given me.

As soon as I walked in, I saw the woman, who must have been Olivia, sitting in a corner booth. She looked just like her aunt, except younger. Same ginger-blonde hair. Same sort of round body shape. Same gentle use of makeup.

She stood up as soon as I started toward her and pulled me into a hug as I reached her. "Paisley, I feel like I know you already," she said as we sat in the booth. "I've read all your newsletters and love the features you sometimes have in the paper. They should give you a regular column."

I blushed under all the attention, but I also appreciated it in a very real way. I worked very hard, and while I still had some remnant of the false humility that so many South-erners carry as a sort of unironic pride, I had learned that kind words were good for my soul and didn't, as many a Sunday school teacher would have had me believe, make me a prideful, arrogant person.

"Why, thank you. We have actually been talking about that," I replied. The paper gig had just come up, spur of the moment, a couple of months back when one of my newslet-ters caught the editor's eye, and she asked if she could run it as a column. Since then, I'd done a piece every few weeks, and the editor was now interested in just what Olivia suggested—a weekly column on historic buildings, families, and events of Octonia.

Olivia bounced a little in her seat. "Oh, that's exciting. I really enjoy what you find out about our home." She leaned forward. "Food first. Then we can really chat."

"Yes, please," I said as I gave the menu a cursory glance and then immediately decided on the same thing I always got. The pimento cheese was that good.

Olivia impressed me by ordering the burger with the egg on it, a sandwich so large that I was pretty sure I'd have to unhinge my jaw like that old flip-top-head toothbrush commercial to eat it. "You're brave," I said to my new acquaintance.

"Ah, my mother has always said I have a big mouth. Might as well put it to good use."

I laughed. "Was it your mom or your dad that was a sibling to Viola?" I had never been good at beating around the bush, so when I saw the opening into my real reason for this meal—besides the pimento cheese—I took it.

"My mom. Victoria." She held my gaze. "Yes, we like our names with a V."

"Hey, you could all be named George, so I say V names are a step up."

Olivia's bark of a laugh echoed around the restaurant and raised several eyebrows. I, however, loved it.

"If you give me that great a reaction for all my lame jokes, I'm going to up my funny game."

"You are one of the funniest writers I've ever read. I laugh out loud at almost every article."

This time, the blush spread hot and fast over my face. I thought I was funny, but my humor wasn't for everyone. I didn't get silly jokes, and physical humor always made me wince. But sarcasm, raw wit. . . those were my strong points.

It was nice to be with someone who appreciated them. "Well, thanks," I said.

"You're welcome," she said as the waitress brought our meals. I would have sworn her burger was purposefully bigger, but she didn't hesitate to open her mouth and fit her teeth around both buns. It really was impressive.

I, however, cut my burger in two and then felt downright dainty when I picked up half, easily took a bite, and didn't even have to wipe my fingers to get cheese off.

We ate in silence for a few minutes before she put down her half-eaten burger and said, "All right, so I know you." She tilted her head. "All right, I don't know you, but I know you research things, so I expect you're researching my aunt's death. How can I help?"

My burger was halfway to my mouth, and I just let it hang there. "What? No, my husband is a police officer. I don't know what you're talking about."

Olivia looked at me from under her eyebrows. "Is this how we're going to play it then?"

I sighed and put my burger down. "Fine. Yes, I'm looking around a bit. But not so much into Viola's murder," I lied, "as into her life." I took a sip of my sweet tea and smiled. "I do like to understand the history of the places I salvage from, and the fact that your family has owned that house for most of its existence is kind of rare."

"It is, I guess. That's really our home place," she said. "But Aunt Viola couldn't keep it when she moved into Grove Manor. It was just too much to manage."

"Well, that answers one question," I said. "I was wondering why she sold, but that makes sense. Grove Manor is really nice, but it's also expensive."

"Best assisted living spot around. And since she was single, she wanted a place she could stay for the rest of her life. They have levels of care, even a hospice ward, so she was all set—" Olivia stopped talking abruptly.

"Gracious. That makes her death even more of a tragedy." The sadness of a life cut short knifed deep into me in that moment. "So, do you know anyone who had something against your aunt?" I asked, trying not to sound like every police drama on TV.

She shook her head. "I've been trying to think about that, but I can't come up with anyone. Even the people she had disagreements with became her friends eventually. She was just that kind of person."

I nodded. "She does sound so lovely." I was very tempted to tell her about the broach, but I had given Santi my word, and while I liked Olivia, I didn't know if she might have had a reason to kill her aunt, like wanting that valuable piece of jewelry for herself. "I keep wondering if it was just a terrible coincidence that she happened to be in the house when someone broke in to loot the place."

Olivia nodded. "That seems the most likely option to me. But why would someone break in? I mean, the house is gorgeous, but unless you're coming with a crowbar"—she winked at me—"there's not much to take that's easily sellable."

I nodded. "She had left a couple of pieces of furniture, but they're pretty much only valuable to someone like me, as you said."

"Yep. They were built to go with the house. My uncle made them."

"Wow. Now, that's a great thing to know." I reached for my purse and then paused. "Do you mind if I take notes?" I didn't want to assume.

She waved a hand. "Please do. I'm an open book."

"So your uncle made the furniture for the house specifically?" I asked as I scribbled. "Was he a furniture maker?"

"Of a sort," she said. "Mostly for friends and family. Sometimes, he sold a couple of pieces, but only on his timeline. He hated deadlines."

I smiled, thinking of my father's similar attitude toward woodworking. "So he made the dining table. What else?" I knew that with these questions, I had sort of sidetracked from the real reason I'd wanted to talk to Olivia, but they would really help me sell the pieces.

She went on to list the built-ins, the small desks we'd found in the bedrooms, as well as a corner cabinet that matched the kitchen cupboards so closely I hadn't even noticed. "If there are any of those pieces you would be willing to sell to me, I'd love to have them," she said quietly, almost as if she was afraid to ask.

"Are you kidding? Those are family heirlooms. Any of them that you want are yours, no charge." I smiled.

"Oh, wow. Would you mind if I got that corner cabinet? I used to keep my toys in there when I was little."

I winced. "Oof, I didn't get that one out of the house because I thought it was one of the fragile cabinets." I paused and thought for a minute. "But if you're free, I could call the new owners and ask if we could go and grab it."

"Are you serious? I'd love that." She pointed one thumb out the front window. "I even have the truck to transport it."

I looked out to see a classic Chevy pickup, probably from the mid-80s, sitting outside the front door. "Perfect," I said. "Manual?"

"Of course," she said. "I wish standards were, well, standard again."

"Same," I said. "Okay, let me check in with the

owners." I stepped outside and immediately got permission to go back in and get the cabinet. Then, I quickly called Santi to give him an update.

"So you're seeing if she responds to the hole behind the sink?" he said with a laugh.

"Well, and getting the cabinet for her, of course," I said, smiling. "But yeah, it seemed fortuitous in a lot of ways to visit the house with her."

"Agreed. I'm out and about today, doing my usual meet and greets, so just call me if you need me." He hung up with a promise to bring dinner home.

"We're all set," I said as I walked back into the restaurant. "I'll just settle—"

"All taken care of," Olivia said as she stood up and put both our tickets on the table. "Least I could do."

I grinned. "Well, thanks. Meet you there?"

She nodded and then hopped into her truck and started the loud engine. It sounded great.

I followed her to the McNamara house and parked on the street while she backed into the driveway like she'd done it a thousand times, which she probably had. Then she walked to a small rock at the corner of the porch, kicked it out of the way, and bent to pick up a key. "Aunt Viola used the same hiding place for years." She handed me the key. "You might want to give this to the new owners."

I laughed. "Well, yeah, I expect they'd like that." I didn't say it, but I expected the Cubbins would be changing the locks if only for aesthetics rather than security concerns. Still, I took the key and used it to open the front door rather than fishing out my set of keys from the depths of my purse with the sunscreen and the bottom half of a chocolate chip muffin.

When Olivia walked in behind me, she paused and took

a deep breath. "Why exactly does everyone's house smell different?" she said quietly.

I shook my head. "I've asked myself the same question so many times. I have no idea, but it's one of the little joys in my work."

Olivia smiled. "What does Aunt Viola's house smell like to you?"

I stood still and took a minute to breathe. "I want to say it smells like cookies, but I think that's more about how I imagine her," I began. "But it smells like something woody, probably the wood itself, and a little bit of mustiness—a smell I love," I clarified. "And then something floral, maybe mums."

"Oh, you're good," Olivia said. "Aunt Viola wore this perfume that always reminded me of fall, but until you said it, I didn't realize it smelled like mums. Thank you," she said as she smiled at me again.

"How about that?" I said. "I may have to add that kind of analysis to my stories. Feels kind of important now that we've talked about it."

She looked down at what had once been the floor. "Maybe we should go around back?"

"Nah, just follow me." I picked my way from floor joist to floor joist all the way to the central hallway, where we hadn't bothered to salvage the floors since the boards were shorter. "See, piece of cake."

"For you, maybe," she said as she walked down the hall.

I tensed a little as she started to walk toward the kitchen. I already knew she was a very observant person, so she was sure to notice the hole above the sink. I wasn't sure whether I wanted her to chalk it up to the demo or to ask about it directly, and my lack of clarity around that fact was puzzling.

I didn't have long to wonder, though, because as soon as I walked in, she said, "Whoa, that's a big hole. Water damage?"

I sighed. I could have nodded and let her believe that, but I had decided honesty really was always the best policy, even if it made things more complicated at first. "Actually, no. Apparently, your aunt used that as a hidey-hole." I had never used the word *hidey-hole* before, but it seemed apt at this moment.

Olivia walked over to the sink and stared into the hole. "Wow. What was she keeping in there?" She turned and looked at me.

It was the moment of truth, and while I wanted to keep my word to Santi, I also wanted to stay honest. "A note from Abe Tuskins, actually." I watched her face as I spoke, and when she registered surprise, I wasn't sure whether I thought that was a good or a bad thing.

"A note from Abe. Really?" She stared at the hole in the wall. "Was it dated?"

Now, that was a good question. "No," I said, "but I assume it was from their courtship, given what you told me about why they broke up."

Olivia nodded. "That would make sense." She looked over at me. "What doesn't make sense is why she kept the note all this time if she was so angry at him."

45

Chapter Five

I took a step back from Olivia and returned her gaze. "She was mad at Abe? I thought you said he was the love of her life."

"He was," she said. "But she was also furious. Okay, maybe not at him per se, but at the situation. He got to go on and become a well-respected judge, and she relied on her parents or her brother for her livelihood her entire life."

I pointed back toward the dining room table as a suggestion we sit. Olivia followed me, and when we were both seated, I asked, "She never worked."

Olivia shook her head. "Never. You know the drill— woman, rural place, and no education. She didn't want to be a teacher or a secretary, so she became one of those women who volunteer for everything."

I thought for a minute about how tired I was some days, about how much I often wished I didn't have to work so hard to make ends meet, especially before Santi and I married. "Some people might think that's nice."

She shrugged. "I guess it's nice if you choose it, but

Aunt Viola wanted to experience the world, travel, and have adventures. Octonia, as you well know, isn't the most exciting place." Olivia looked up at me as one corner of her mouth turned up. "Unless, of course, you find dead bodies all the time."

I rolled my eyes but was glad she was teasing. "I can see what you mean. So, Viola just accepted financial help from her family? I think I'd resent that."

"Oh, she did, but her father was unwilling to pay for her to go to any sort of school, and when her father died and her brother took over her bills, she thought it was too late. She was in her 60s and just didn't think she had enough time left."

I groaned. "I hate that for her. Man." I looked around the room we were in. "So this house was really everything to her?"

"Everything. She kept it immaculate, and you should have seen the garden."

"I noticed the snowdrops out front," I said, thinking back to my first visit with Sawyer.

Olivia smiled. "The whole yard is full of bulbs. Give it a couple of weeks, and it's going to be gorgeous, even unkempt."

"Oh, that sounds lovely. I'll make sure the new owners know." I paused a minute, conflicted by the fact that I really liked the Cubbins but also felt like the house belonged, in some deep way, to the McNamara's. "Do you want to meet them?"

Olivia studied my face. "If you think they'd be open to that, I'd love it, but the house is theirs now. I want them to feel comfortable making it their own." She spoke without pause, but I could hear the strain in her voice.

From the way the Cubbins had come in ready to renovate, I didn't get the sense they'd be put off by talking to Olivia. They seemed quite comfortable with the fact that they held the title and had even paid for the house in cash, so they didn't have to pay a mortgage. It was clearly theirs.

"I don't think they'd mind at all," I said. "Obviously, they're into history since they hired me. Maybe dinner at my place? Tomorrow night?"

"Ooh, I'm going to get to see the famous farmhouse and site of your wedding?"

I laughed. "It's not that glamorous, but yes, of course. I do ask guests to stop and pay their respects at the graveyard, though." I'd recently invited neighbors to inter their ancestors in our yard since their bodies had been found there. The story and the graveyard had been county news for a while.

"Of course. May I bring flowers?"

"Absolutely. I'll reach out to the Cubbins and see if they're available. Just be forewarned, Sawyer will be there, and he loves an adult who comes without a kid." I smiled, hoping that my new friend wouldn't balk at the presence of my young child like some people did.

"In that case, mind if I bring a kid of my own? Jade is seven and loves a good romp."

"Oh, I'm so sorry. Yes, of course, bring your... daughter? Son? Child?"

"Cocker Spaniel, actually. Yep, I'm one of those people who call their pets their children." She grinned at me. "She's well-behaved and loves kids."

"That sounds perfect, then. I'll just be sure Beauregard is well-supplied upstairs since he is not as well-behaved." I winced as I remembered the last time my cat had met a dog. The dog definitely got the worst end of that deal.

"Oh, I don't have to bring her if it's troub—"

"No trouble at all. Beau doesn't like to be around guests much anyway. He'll be quite content to be disgruntled upstairs alone." Until Santi and I went to bed. Then, he'd show his ire, but Olivia didn't need to know that.

She smiled at me. "Well, should we get this cabinet out of here?" She glanced back toward the front of the house.

I laughed. "We can go out the back door this time."

Later that evening, over dinner, I told Sawyer and Santi all about my meeting with Olivia. Saw was, of course, excited to meet Jade, and Santi expressed an unusual amount of interest in Olivia and her history with the house. "So she basically grew up there?" he asked.

I looked at him as he shoveled a mouthful of green beans into his mouth. "I don't know that I'd go that far, but it does sound like she spent a lot of time there as a kid. I was glad she got to have the cabinet."

Santi nodded. "Remind me to ask you something about that later." He shot a significant look over at Sawyer to tell me why he wasn't asking now.

"Okay," I said. "Sawyer, how was school?" I wasn't very subtle about my subject change, but Saw was too young and too excited to care.

"Ms. Odettly, that's my teacher," he said with all serious-ness as he nodded to us like we wouldn't know. "She's getting a class hamster, and she said we can all take turns bringing it home for the weekend."

I sighed. "Oh, really, is that what Ms. Odettly said."

"Yep, and since I helped with cleanup after art today, I get the first turn."

"You do?" I tried to sound excited, but all I could think about was having to feed a hamster over the weekend.

Santi winked at me. "Did you talk to your dad about that, Saw?"

Sawyer studied him. "No."

"Well, you spend weekends at your dad's house, so the hamster will need to go to his house. Think you better ask?" Santi's face was serious.

"Oh, yeah," Saw said. "Mom, can I borrow your phone?"

My son had just learned how to unlock my phone, and since his father's name was marked with a car picture, he didn't need my help to make the call.

"Take the phone into the living room, love bug," I said as I began to clear the plates.

As Santi and I began to wash up, we could hear Sawyer's excited babbling at his father about the hamster. "Quick, what did you want to ask me about the cabinet?" I said, far too impatient to wait for a later time.

Santi glanced toward the living room, where Sawyer had gone quiet for a moment. We both waited, and when Saw began talking again, Santi said, "Did you search it?"

I looked over at my husband, who was washing dishes as I put away leftovers. "What do you think?"

"I think you might not have had the chance," he said as he flicked bubbles at me.

I wiggled my hips. "I have my ways, Sheriff. And yes, I did. It was clean."

He stepped over and put a bit of soap on my nose. "Smart woman, you."

After I picked Sawyer up from school the next day, I rushed home to meet Santi and get dinner prepped. We had set five for the time because of Sawyer's schedule, and it turned out that it was ideal for the Cubbins since they wanted to go to a play at the Octonia Theater that evening. As an introvert who finds groups kind of awkward sometimes, I liked this kind of gathering, especially with people I didn't know well. An ending time always puts me a bit more at ease.

When a sleek Tesla pulled into my driveway at five on the dot, I assumed it held Dolores and Peter Cubbins and went out to greet them. A woman stepped out from behind the wheel and immediately extended her hand. "Paisley, thank you for having us over. I'm Dolores." She gestured across the car. "And this is Peter. Your house is lovely."

I smiled as she took in the open lawns around the farm-house's various outbuildings and then looked down the hill toward the graveyard that we had carefully surrounded by a classic wrought-iron fence.

"May we pay our respects?" Peter asked as he handed me a bottle of wine. "Dolores informed me of your policy."

"Of course, please do." I heard gravel on the drive and looked up to see Olivia pulling in. "I'll walk down with Olivia in just a moment."

The couple began the stroll through the yard, and I noticed that while they were both wearing expensive cloth-ing, it was also practical—boat shoes and khakis. So they were wealthy but not ridiculous. I could respect that.

"Hi there," I said as Olivia hopped down. "And this must be Jade." The floppy-eared dog was panting and wagging her short tail with abandon as I bent down to let her sniff my fingers and give her ears a rub. "The Cubbins just went down to the graveyard. I suggested we'd join them."

Olivia smiled. "Perfect." She let Jade lead the way on her rainbow-colored leash, and soon, all five of us were at the graves, standing silently. Olivia laid flowers by both of the stones, and I told everyone a bit about the people buried there before we headed back up to the house.

As soon as we went inside, Sawyer politely said hello and then asked if he could take Jade outside to play. "I'm very good with dogs," he said earnestly.

"Absolutely," Olivia said. "You can even let her off her leash if you promise to keep her in sight or get me if she starts to run away."

"I can do that," he said, then led the bouncing dog outside.

"They'll both be exhausted soon," I said. "Thanks for bringing Jade over." I handed around glasses of wine as everyone stood in the kitchen and introduced themselves.

Soon, stories about growing up in Octonia were flying. Peter had spent his childhood summers here up on the edge of the mountains at his parents' cabin, and of course, Santi, Olivia, and I had all grown up here. Only Dolores didn't have lifelong memories of our area, but she seemed to enjoy hearing about ours thoroughly.

The lasagna I'd made was ready a bit later, and while I refilled glasses and got everyone seated at the table, Santi went to fetch boy and dog, who had both found a glorious mudhole and required a good scrubbing before dinner. Fortunately, Saw was good with washing his hands—germs were his nemesis—and Jade was tired enough to enjoy lying on the concrete porch until I could get a towel to clean her off.

I loved a family-style dinner with friends, and it was a joy to hear everyone complimenting my lasagna, taking seconds on Santi's garlic bread, and praising the cucumbers that Sawyer had raised in our greenhouse.

"A family meal is so nice," Dolores said as she took more lasagna. "It's not something I had growing up." She turned to Olivia. "But I expect you all had some great meals around that dining room table at your aunt's place."

I appreciated Dolores's gentle shift in our conversation to bring us to the reason for our gathering. I'd been trying to figure out how to talk about the house and Ms. McNamara gracefully, and I was glad I wasn't just going to have to say something like, "So let's talk about Viola."

"Oh yes, every Saturday night. It was usually a big potluck, and Aunt Viola always made fried chicken. We'd eat ourselves sick and then play Rook until the wee hours of the morning. The kids would fall asleep all over the house until their parents carried them to the car and home to bed." She sighed. "It was kind of perfect."

"Sounds like it," Peter said. "Tell us a bit more about your aunt, if you would. Then we'd like to ask for your help with something."

Olivia looked at him closely and said, "Aunt Viola was a force. She had to be. Life had dealt her some really hard blows, and she was a woman before feminism really brought any change." She paused and studied her fingernails. "She could have just settled down, kept to herself, but she didn't. She was the person who spear-headed getting Gloria Steinhem's work at the local library."

"Oh, tell me more about that," Dolores said.

Olivia launched into an epic tale of book burnings at the courthouse and death threats because of Steinem's woman-centered thinking. "But Aunt Viola didn't back down, and she eventually rallied enough women in town to request the book that they flooded the librarian's mailbox and got her to agree, even if it meant she might lose some funding."

"Did she lose funding?" Santi asked.

"Oh yeah, the board of supervisors refused to fund the library until Steinem's books were removed." Olivia grinned. "But that didn't stop the women of Octonia. They just ponied up the funds themselves."

"Holy cow, I love your aunt," I blurted before realizing that such enthusiasm over the woman whose body I found might not be appropriate.

"Me, too," Olivia said. "She was amazing. But that's what I don't understand. I can't think of a single soul who would want to hurt her." Her face fell.

Dolores reached over and put her hand on Olivia's. "We feel partially responsible since it happened in our house." She sat up straighter. "We don't know why she was there, though. Do you have any idea?" She studied Olivia's face for a long moment.

"No idea," Olivia said. "Except that maybe she went back for the note."

"The note and the broach," Santi added.

I looked at him quickly, and he nodded. He had mentioned the broach on purpose, so he was up to something.

"The broach? What broach?" Olivia asked.

"Since it was part of an ongoing investigation, I couldn't tell you without the sheriff's permission." I squeezed Santi's knee under the table. "But we found a Christmas tree pin with Abe Tuskins' note."

Olivia stared at me for a long moment and then shook her head. "A pin of a Christmas tree? My aunt didn't really wear jewelry."

I opened my phone and pulled up the photo of the pin

that I'd snapped when we found it. "You don't recognize this?" I said as I held it out to Olivia.

She leaned in to look at the picture but shook her head. "Not at all."

I turned the camera so Dolores and Peter could see it. "And this isn't yours, correct?"

Santi bumped my leg under the table, a little warning not to go too far with my questions.

Both of them shook their heads. "Definitely not ours."

Olivia looked at Dolores and then grinned. "Too tacky, right?"

Dolores laughed. "Well, I wasn't going to say anything."

"Oh no, it's okay. That thing is hideous. Are those even real stones?" She looked at the picture again.

"The rubies are real," Santi said. "And so is the gold. The emeralds are paste, though."

"What, real rubies?" Olivia said as she snatched the phone out of my hand. "How much is it worth?"

"Over $25,000," Santi answered.

Peter let out a low wolf whistle. "Wow."

Santi looked from him back to Olivia. "Technically, it belongs to the Cubbins. . ." he paused to give them a chance to speak.

"Oh no, that's certainly Olivia's," Dolores said as she looked at her nodding husband. "If it was your aunt's, it belongs to you."

Olivia stared at them for a long moment. "What? No. It was in your house."

"Nope, we insist," Dolores said. "Your aunt hid that in the wall for a reason." She turned to Santi. "Do you think she came back for it? Is that why she was in the house?"

The Cubbins already knew this was our working theory,

but I appreciated the way they gentled Olivia into that possibility.

"We think that is probably the case. Tomorrow, I'm going to talk with Abe Tuskins to see if he knows anything about the broach," Santi continued.

Olivia's eyes went wide. "You think the note and the broach go together? Like he gave her that pin?"

I shrugged. "We'll have to see."

"But he was Jewish," Olivia said.

"Your aunt wasn't, though," Santi added.

"Whoa." Olivia sat completely still for a long moment. "All right then."

"You understand that we can't give you the broach just yet since it's part of an active murder investigation," Santi said as he stood to bring out the banana cream pie he'd bought for dessert.

Olivia shook her head as if to clear it. "Oh, of course. I don't even know if I want it." I saw tears pooling in her eyes.

"Why not?" Dolores said as she moved to comfort the younger woman. "You obviously loved your aunt, and she obviously treasured that pin."

"Did she, though?" Olivia said quietly. "Do you wall something up and hide it if you love it?"

I had to admit she had a fair point. It seemed like Viola would have worn the broach or at least had it in a place of honor in her room if she really loved it.

"No, I don't think I want it. If it turns out you don't need it for the investigation, Sheriff Shifflett, I'll sell it and donate the money." Olivia's voice was firm as she stood up.

"Thank you for having me over, Paisley." She turned to the Cubbins. "It was nice to meet both of you, and you," she said as she shook Santi's hand. "Please let me know if I can help you with anything about the house," she said to Dolores as she picked up her bag. "Good night."

Her departure was so abrupt that the four of us sat silently, staring at the door after she left. Finally, though, Santi said, "Well, who wants pie?"

Still, the intensity of Olivia's reaction to the news of the pin left a lingering weight on the evening, and soon after she left, Dolores and Peter followed suit.

After everyone left, Santi and I went into cleanup mode, both brooding in our heads as we wiped up and put things away. When we were done, it was time to put Sawyer to bed, so I stepped onto the porch and called down to his treehouse, where I could see his little head bobbing around as he acted out some pretend saga.

"Coming, Mom," he replied.

I turned back to wait for him in the house when I heard the distinctive sound of a bark coming from behind me. When I looked back, Sawyer and Jade were running toward me. Olivia had left her dog here.

Chapter Six

I tried to call Olivia as soon as we realized Jade was still at our house, but she didn't pick up or answer my texts. I was worried. She had seemed bothered when she left but not bothered enough to forget her dog.

Still, there wasn't much I could do about it since I didn't know where she lived. Instead, I decided to test Sawyer a little in animal care and told him what he needed to do for Jade before bed. The boy gave the dog some of Beauregard's cat food with a raw egg, a bowl of water, and a walk around the yard before he went to bed—which he did, of course, with Jade. When I checked on them a few minutes after I said good night, they were sound asleep with their heads on Saw's pillow. It was pretty adorable.

I snapped a picture and texted it over to Olivia. "She's in good hands," I wrote. "Let us know how we can get her to you."

I checked my phone approximately every thirty-two seconds for the next two hours, but Olivia never replied. Just before ten, I gave her another call, but she didn't pick up.

"Still not answering?" Santi said as we climbed into bed.

"No. It's weird, right?"

"To forget your dog? Yes, that's weird." He rolled over and looked at me. "You don't think she left her here on purpose, do you?"

I would have been lying to say that the idea hadn't occurred to me. "I don't know."

"Tomorrow, I'll find her address and stop by. See if I can figure out what's up."

"Thanks," I said, giving him a kiss. "Sheriff Returns Lost Pup—it would make a great news story."

Santi laughed as he shut off the light.

The next day, though, didn't bring any new information on Jade or her owner. Santi went by her apartment just outside of town, but no one answered. The neighbors said they hadn't seen her since the day before. "It isn't like her," one woman told him. "She's always sitting out here on the stoop, talking with folks."

"So are we now considering Olivia missing?" I asked my husband when he called after his visit.

"Not technically, no. She hasn't even been gone twenty-four hours, and we don't really have any reason to suspect anyone did anything to her." He sighed. "But that doesn't mean I'm not going to keep looking. No living family, right?"

"That's what I gather," I said. "Partner? Friends?"

"Neighbors didn't see her with anyone and definitely not with the same person several times," Santi said.

"Should I let the Cubbins know since they were some of

the last people to see her?" I figured it was a long shot, but it couldn't hurt.

"Actually, yeah. Put out the word, would you? Maybe she's just out getting drunk or something? Someone might have seen her."

"Will do. No restrictions on who I can ask?" My husband and I had very different definitions of private. Mine rounded out near where most people used the word *public*.

"Not a one." He hung up with a promise to see Saw and me for dinner, and I got to work. First, I posted about Olivia on Facebook, asking people to let the sheriff know if they had seen her. Then I called Mary and Mika and asked them to share my post and ask around. Finally, I called my dad and stepmom. They were connected to the older Octonia set—those folks who didn't really use social media and relied on actual conversations to learn things.

"I'll make some calls," Dad said. "I'll ask Lucille to as well." He cleared his throat. "This have anything to do with that woman's body you found?"

My dad was a big supporter of my work but didn't love that I got wrapped up in murder investigations with a fair amount of regularity. "It's the victim's niece," I said. "We only really know she's gone, though, because she came for supper and left her dog here."

"She left her dog?" Dad said. "Sounds like she might not be coming back."

It wasn't that I hadn't thought the same thing, but still, my stomach dropped. "Yeah," I said. "Could be."

"Alrighty then, I'll let you know if we hear anything." He hung up without another word. Typical Dad.

By the time I went to pick up Sawyer at school, I was getting regular pings on my Facebook post and not a few text messages asking if anyone had seen Olivia. I replied to each one to say we hadn't and asked people to keep looking.

Jade rode along with me to the elementary school building, and when Sawyer saw she was in the car, he sprinted across the sidewalk, prompting several calls of "No running" from teachers staffing pickup.

"Oh, Jade, you're still here. Does this mean I get to keep her?" he said.

I shook my head as I realized I was feeling not a small amount of anger at Olivia for doing this to my child. If she didn't come back soon, Sawyer would be devastated when Jade had to leave. "No, love bug. We're just watching her for Olivia for a while."

He frowned but quickly perked up when Jade licked the full length of his face. "Can Jade and I play outside when we get home?"

"I think that's a stellar idea," I said. "Maybe she'll play fetch."

The three of us spent the better part of two hours running around the yard on what was a pleasantly warm spring afternoon. Jade was very good at fetching but absolutely abhorrent at returning the ball, so Sawyer wore himself out chasing her down to get the ball from her and then did it all over again.

I had to admit, the pup was kind of growing on me, too. But my worry for her owner was outpacing my affection for the cocker spaniel. I just couldn't figure out what was going on.

For the next two days, Santi and I kept our hunt up for Olivia, but when Friday rolled around with no word from her, he officially declared her a missing person and took the search wider. Meanwhile, we still had a cocker spaniel in our care, *and* our son had just brought home the classroom hamster, Hoover. Fortunately, the hamster was going with my son to his father's house for the weekend, so we were just left babysitting a young woman's dog.

That job was profoundly simple once the wild child was out of the house. Apparently, Jade was exhausted, and as soon as Sawyer left, she curled up on the dog bed that Santi had bought her and went to sleep—and snored. That dog snored like she was a lumberjack.

Beauregard, who had assiduously avoided Jade for the entire week, now decided she was worthy of attention and spent a considerable amount of time batting at her ears while she slept. He eventually gave up, probably because she didn't react, and curled up next to her. It was almost as cute as Sawyer and the dog sleeping together. Almost.

Things had been steady at the store, and my store manager, Claire, had been great at keeping things restocked. But she'd sent me a text on Friday to let me know we were starting to get sparse in our smaller offerings. I told her I'd bring some things out of storage, which meant I had to actually go and get them from storage.

Fortunately, Ms. Stephenson was working at the yarn store for Mika, so Mika and I got up early, headed to the diner for breakfast, and then went to Saul's shipping container at the back of his construction lot to retrieve the trinkets I'd put there when it became clear I was gathering faster than I was selling. Saul had insisted I use the space because "It's always better to have the supply when there is the demand than to come up empty-handed."

He was right. Here I was, not two months after I'd packed all this away, pulling out the huge boxes of taxider-mied animals I'd gotten at a steal from an antique sale. I had no idea why anyone loved these things—I found them sad and a little gross—but they sold really well, especially if the animal was unusual. And I had unusual—an aardvark, a male peacock, and a family of naked molerats. Those mole rats were so ugly when they were alive, and when stuffed, they were downright terrifying.

"Seriously, Pais, these are amazing," my best friend said as she studied the small family of rodents mounted on a wooden platform. "If you'd charge me full price, I'd buy them for the store."

I shivered. "No, you can't buy them because I don't want to cringe every time I come into your store. Besides, you don't need any more stuffed animals." Mika had read *Furiously Happy* by Jenny Lawson, who owned at least one stuffed raccoon, and had insisted that if I ever saw one, I had to buy it for her. I'd given her my word and had, sadly, come upon one rather quickly. Now, it sat next to her cash register with a plate of pennies in its hands for customers. *Ick.*

"So, still no word on Olivia?" Mika asked as she pulled down several acorn-shaped corbels and selected a couple of scrolled newel posts for us to display.

"Nothing. She apparently lived a pretty solitary life. Santi hasn't been able to find any friends or even distant cousins," I said as I put two pewter scones on the pile we were making. "That's so sad," Mika said, "but then, maybe she wasn't sad. Maybe she liked the solitary life."

"Likes the solitary life. Likes it—present tense. She's not dead." Even as I said the words, I wished I hadn't.

"Let's hope not."

We loaded up my car and drove back out to the front of the lot where the old farmhouse that served as my retail shop was located. It wasn't yet nine in the morning, so we weren't open. I'd given Claire the weekend off so she could attend her sister's wedding, which meant I was staffing the store. I planned to get the biggest new items out before we opened, and then I would spend the day fiddling with the little things as I redid some displays around the shop.

Mika and I got the peacock and the aardvark set out on a high shelf, away from curious little fingers, and then arranged corbels and newel posts by the fireplace down-stairs. By then, it was time to open, and when I flipped the sign on the window, I saw several people were already wait-ing. We'd become part of the yard sale/flea market route of late, and it meant bargain seekers were always chomping at the bit for new finds on a weekend morning.

Fortunately, I had planned ahead for them and had significantly marked down a few items—including a black canvas pram—to give them the thrill of finding a good deal. The pram and its compadres had been taking up space on my main floor for too long, and I was really glad to see a woman with bright red hair rush for the stroller as soon as she got in the door.

We were well into a good morning of sales when Dolores Cubbins came in. She made her way around the room the cash register was in and eventually stopped near where I was helping a customer buy the naked mole rats. They sold at a premium, which was good, but I was more than happy just to see them sold, period.

After the customer left, grinning and talking to his new "pets," Dolores approached. "Do you have a minute?" she asked in a whisper.

"Sure," I said. "Mika, do you mind?"

When my best friend nodded and raised one eyebrow until I shook my head, she quickly moved to take over at the register. I led Dolores upstairs to my office, a front-facing bedroom filled with my favorite collection of strange items accented with hot pink, orange, and teal. I had come to brighter colors in middle age, and there was no going back.

We sat side by side on the teal loveseat against the side wall, and I turned to her, my legs folded under me. "Is everything okay?" I asked.

Dolores let out a heavy sigh. "I don't know, and I didn't know who to talk with about it."

She met my eyes. "I understand that you might want to talk about this with your husband, but perhaps you'll think about my husband before you decide?"

"What about your husband?"

"I found this," she said as she pulled a folded piece of paper out of her purse and handed it to me.

I opened it to see a printout of an online auction listing for a Christmas tree pin that looked remarkably like the one I had found in their kitchen wall. "I don't understand," I said.

"I found this in Peter's pocket yesterday." She took the paper back. "I don't know what it means, but it made me nervous."

I smiled. "Maybe he's just curious about the broach?" I noticed this one was selling for $10,000, which wasn't worth what the one we'd found was because this wasn't a Cartier piece.

"Maybe," she said with a shrug. "But why not talk to me about it then? Why look it up and tuck this away?"

"He forgot?" I said, trying to come up with an explanation that would satisfy her. "I would probably have looked it up, too. I'm just a curious person."

"And that's just it," she said. "Peter is not. He doesn't read. He's not interested in history. Mostly, he just likes to garden and tinker in his shop. He doesn't even do research for his job."

I nodded. "What is his job?"

"He's a loan officer at a bank," she said. "This just isn't like him."

I wasn't one to dismiss the concerns of a spouse about their partner. After all, we were the ones who almost always knew our partners best, but in this case, it felt like Dolores was overreacting. "Is there anything else?" People didn't come to acquaintances with concerns about their spouses over one internet search.

She shrugged again. "That's the thing. He's just been too interested in this whole situation. He even went over to the house today to look at where you found the note and broach."

"He did?" Now, I did find that odd since, as far as I knew, the Cubbins hadn't been in their new home since they checked it before closing. The realtor had told me they just wanted to have the remodeling done before they even saw the place again.

"That's weird, right?" She spun her wedding ring. "He said he wanted to see what kind of repair the wall would need, but that doesn't make any sense—"

"Because they're going to tear all the walls out, right?"

"Exactly. I suggested I could go with him, but he told me to enjoy my day and spend it doing what I loved. He didn't want to bore me with house stuff." She threw her hands up. "All of it could be so normal—he really is a considerate guy like that—but something feels off."

I studied her for a minute. "Well, something is off, right? A woman was murdered in your new home. Maybe he's just working through that fact in his own way?" I wasn't sure how much I believed what I was saying, but it felt best to give her reassurance without something more tangible to acknowledge her suspicions.

Dolores smiled. "You may be right." She sat back against the loveseat. "Do you think you could take me there? Maybe tomorrow? Peter will be golfing with friends, and now I feel like I need to see the house again to remind myself of why we bought it."

I smiled. "Sure. Ten in the morning work for you. I can meet you there?"

"Thank you," she said. "Sorry to bother you with this, but I didn't know who else would understand."

I walked with her down the stairs. "No worries at all. I completely get it. See you tomorrow."

As soon as Dolores was out the door, Mika came over. "What was that all about?"

"Well, I'm not sure, but I think we now have two suspects in Viola McNamara's murder."

I thought for all of two minutes about not telling Santi what had just happened, but I knew I wouldn't feel good about myself if I didn't tell him. Secrets had meant nothing but pain in my life.

I texted him and asked him to stop by the shop when he could. I didn't think anything Dolores had said was urgent, so there was no need to pull him away from the yard work at our house unnecessarily. That mulch needed spreading, after all.

When he showed up in the middle of the afternoon, freshly showered and smelling like pine and sandalwood, I grinned. He looked amazing, and I couldn't believe I had the privilege of being his wife. His black hair was just graying at the temples, and he had the best laugh lines around his eyes. He was the most handsome man I'd ever seen.

"How's business?" he said after kissing my cheek.

"Slow now, but we had a good morning." I smiled at him. "Too bad you're all clean because I have a couple of chandeliers I was going to ask you to help me hang."

"Oh, so that's why you asked me to stop by. Manual labor." He laughed. "I'm happy to help."

"Actually, that's not why I asked. Dolores Cubbins came by."

"Oh?" he said, moving toward the wrought-iron chandelier I had placed in the middle of the room. "What did she want?"

As we hung the chandelier, I told him about Dolores's visit. "Nothing she said seemed that odd to me, but her reaction was intense."

"And you're not sure if you're more worried about what her husband might be doing or what she's up to?" He stepped down from the ladder and surveyed his handiwork, which was perfect, of course.

"This is why I married you."

"Well, you know what they say about great minds," he said, kissing my cheek. "Want me to come tomorrow when you take her to the house?"

I thought about that for a minute. "No," I said. "I think that would scare her. But maybe I'll take Mika along."

"Good idea. Maybe then you guys can get that table you've been talking about all week?"

"Oh, that's a good idea." At first, I had decided against taking the table, and I'd even thought about offering it to

Olivia before she disappeared. But now, I could see that piece sitting right in the middle of this room. It could be a place for customers to relax, for us to have staff meetings, and even be a centerpiece for a holiday gathering for Saul and his crew. I couldn't let it go, and I had probably mentioned it to Santi about fifteen times.

The next morning, I picked Mika up from her apartment over her store and drove to the McNamara house. We were a little early, mostly to scope out how we'd get the table out of the dining room. I was hoping the legs would easily unscrew so that we could take it in pieces to the pickup Dom was bringing over later.

Fortunately for us, in more ways than one, the table was constructed entirely from pegs with no screws, nails, or glue in sight. So we just had to tap out the pegs—easier said than done in some spots—and take the parts out back for the guys to pick up later.

We were done by the time Dolores arrived at ten, and I was glad to have the table ready to go just in case things went wonky with her visit. In my experience, most home-owners weren't at all attached to the old things in a house unless they were history buffs like me. And I wasn't too worried that Dolores, with her very modern sensibilities, would be interested in the table anyway. But this way, it wasn't even a question.

We met her on the front porch to walk into the house with her—a fact that Santi had stressed was important so we could watch her reactions—and guide her over the joists into the back part of the building. I was beginning to regret pulling up the floor.

To her credit, Dolores didn't miss a beat when step-leaping from joist to joist, and when we got to the dining room and kitchen, now even barer than before, she simply stood and looked at the space. "This is where you found the poor woman?" she asked.

"Yes," I said, unwilling to go into any more detail in order to protect Santi's investigation. "And that's where we found the note and the broach." I pointed toward the hole above the sink.

Dolores walked over and peered inside. "Not much to see, is there?"

Mika rolled her eyes at me.

"Nope. Just a hole," I said. "But I get why you wanted to see it yourself. I think I asked you this before," I said, "but did Ms. McNamara contact you about coming to visit the house on the day she died?" I knew very well that the Cubbins had both said they'd not seen the woman except at the closing, but sometimes, stories changed on a second query.

Mrs. Cubbins's tale held, though. "No, she never contacted us." She paused. "But maybe she asked the realtor and got the code from her like you did?"

Now, there was a possibility I hadn't considered. "That's a good question. Would you mind asking her?"

Mika shot me a sharp look, and I gave her a subtle shake of my head.

"Don't mind at all. I'll call her as soon as we're done here and let you know," Dolores said. "Well, I don't know what I was hoping for, but I guess this is what I get."

I raised my hands in an exaggerated shrug. "Would you mind telling us about what you're having done for the remodel?"

At this question, Dolores's face lit up. "I'd love to."

Then, for the next thirty minutes, she walked us through every room—or in the case of the living room, she pointed us through it—telling us about design features and wall removals, even down to the kind of light switches and door knobs they would be installing. As best I could tell, everything would be gray and white, which I thought sounded barren and stark. Dolores, however, seemed very excited, and I didn't want to dampen her spirits with my remarks about trends and the need for homes to feel lived in.

After her tour, Dolores headed back out to the front door, moving over the joists effortlessly, and promised to let me know what the realtor said posthaste.

As soon as the door closed behind her, Mika spun toward me. "Don't you think you should ask the realtor yourself in case she lies?"

"Already did," I said to Mika as I held up my phone. "You didn't really think I was paying attention the whole time she went on about polished versus brushed nickel in the bathroom, did you?"

Mika laughed. "I should never think something has gotten past you, Pais. You've got it all under control."

Somehow, I really doubted that.

Chapter Seven

The realtor responded to my text just moments after Mrs. Cubbins left. She said Ms. McNamara had indeed contacted her, and Mr. Cubbins had given permission for the former owner to take one last walk-through. So apparently, Viola had let herself in with the lockbox code, and that was why there wasn't any sign of a break-in.

"So that's how she got in, but what about the person who killed her?" Mika asked as we waited on the front porch for *Dom* and Santi to arrive.

"I imagine she left the door unlocked, don't you think?" I suggested.

"I guess. My parents still don't lock their doors."

"Mine neither. I don't think my dad knows where the keys to his house are," I added with a nervous laugh. "Maybe I should talk to him about that."

"Maybe," Mika said. "So, walk me through what you're thinking."

I looked at her carefully. "What do you mean?"

"Oh, you know what I mean. Who are your suspects?"

I rolled my eyes. "I don't have suspects. That's Santi's job."

"And I haven't known you since college. Please."

"All right, so I guess I'd say it's now both the Cubbins and Olivia, but if the motive were to get the broach and steal it, then they would have had to know about it. All of them seemed really surprised at the news," I said as I processed what had been dancing around at the back of my mind for days now. "The thing is, I don't know how anyone would have known about the pin. I wouldn't have even found it if I hadn't been taking tiles off the wall."

"Well, there's a question—were the tiles loose?" Mika said.

I pondered the question for a minute. "I'm not sure. I had a rhythm, and I was just popping tiles off. Some of them came easily; others didn't. But since I didn't know I was going to come upon a hidey-hole—"

"You really like that term, huh?" Mika said with a laugh.

"I do," I said. "I've never had reason to use it before, so I'm going to get a lifetime's worth of use in now."

She laughed. "Sorry, what were you saying?"

"Just that since I wasn't expecting a hole, I didn't really take special note of the tiles above it."

"Fair enough," Mika said. "But that does mean they might have been easy to take on and off if you knew where to look."

I nodded. "I guess so."

Just then, the guys pulled up, and Mika pointed them around back, where we quickly loaded the table into the bed.

"Hey, *Dom*," I asked, "you know anything about laying tile?"

He looked at me in askance. "Not particularly. Why?"

I told him and Santi about Mika's theory on the tiles.

"You know, there's one way we might be able to find out," Santi said.

I poked out my head and said, "What's that?"

"By going through the tiles we salvaged," he said with a wry grin. "I'll order pizza."

So that is how the four of us ended up unloading the truck and then looking at the backside of hundreds of pieces of black and white tile on the floor of the front room in my shop. Fortunately, the mortar, or whatever substance was used to attach tile, was pretty consistent throughout the pieces, so when we found two that had nothing at all on the back, we noticed instantly.

"You were right," I said to Mika. "These weren't glued down."

Mika grinned. "I think you're rubbing off on me."

"Oh no, another one," Santi said with a wink at *Dom*.

"Lord, help us all," he said.

"You know what this means then?" I said with a glance at my three friends. "Viola could have shown anyone the note and the broach at any time. They were hidden but not inaccessible."

"Were they dusty when you pulled them out?" *Dom* asked.

I tried to think back. "Not that I can remember."

Santi shook his head. "I don't remember you wiping them off or anything."

Mika jumped up from the floor. "So they were put there recently!" she said, pointing one finger in the air.

"All right, Clouseau," Santi said, "We don't know that for sure. They could have been there a long time but were taken out regularly."

I sighed. "I guess we can at least safely assume they hadn't been in there untouched for that long."

"That does seem likely," Santi said.

We all grew quite as we began to refill boxes with the tiles we'd just sorted. It felt like we'd figured out something important but not how it was important. That feeling was almost more frustrating than not knowing anything.

Finally, after we'd put everything away and Dom and Mika had headed out to the movies, I said, "I think I need to talk to Abe Tuskins again."

"Oh no, my dear. It's time for me to speak to the man. I'll do it tomorrow." Santi studied me for a minute and then grinned. "But maybe you could make the introduction."

I laughed. "Of course."

He looked at his watch. "Now, let's get home and meet that boy of ours. He's going to need at least a good two hours of constant talking to wind down enough for sleep."

Santi wasn't wrong. Sawyer came back all keyed up from a fun weekend with his dad and had tales to tell, including a scary incident with Hoover the hamster and the back of the kitchen range. Fortunately, Hoover was a chubby fellow and had gotten himself stuck as he tried to wedge his way through an opening at the back of the oven. He then squeaked himself silly until Sawyer and his father found him and put him back in his comfy cage. "He didn't even run in his wheel all weekend," Saw said. "He had used up all his energy."

"I'd have probably slept a lot, too, if I'd had that kind of adventure," Santi said.

"Trust me, you would have," I said, remembering my narrow crawl on one of my first salvage jobs. "Those adventures will tucker you out."

On Monday, Sawyer went to school after eating six pieces of salami, a yogurt, and two tangerines. I packed him a couple more oranges for snacks and hoped that lunch was ready for his teenage-like appetite. Then I put him on the bus and watched with delight as he jabbered away to a kid with an amazing afro in the seat next to him. He was good.

And I was good, at least I thought so. I had slept well, and when I woke up, I had a new idea for my next newsletter—a history of the craftsman cottage with the McNamara place as a model. I'd taken lots of pictures before we'd salvaged, and I figured those would interest readers. Plus, I hoped we might also get some more information about Viola McNamara from readers.

Santi left for work early but had promised to let me know the timing of his interview with Abe Tuskins. So, I had plenty of time to write and get a little help with my research.

Xzanthia Lewis answered the phone at the historical society on the first ring. The director was a dear friend, and I knew that if anyone could find information about Viola McNamara, maybe even about the broach, she could.

As soon as I filled her in on the situation, she said, "First, I have a friend who specializes in costume jewelry. Let me call her. Then, I'll look through our archives. Want to join me?"

"Give me an hour?" I asked. If at all possible, I never turned down a chance to dig into the county archives or to spend time with Xzanthia, for that matter. She was a strong woman, one I admired, and she knew more about Octonia than anyone else I knew.

My newsletter only took a few minutes to write up since

I loaded it with pictures and links to inform my readers about the history of the craftsman style. In the end, I included a brief note on Viola McNamara and her parents, the home's original owners, and told my readers I was eager to learn more about them if they had more to share.

I was also hoping that maybe Olivia was out there, laying low for some reason that I couldn't understand but wanted to think was about safety and not hiding, and might respond to the newsletter. I didn't have high hopes, but a little hope sometimes went a long way.

With the newsletter scheduled to go out at eleven, the prime time for my readers according to all those tools that measure things I don't understand, I headed to town and parked right in front of the historical society.

The morning was gorgeous, just warm enough in the sun to be pleasant. Xzanthia was on the front porch with her laptop and a box of files, and when I sat down, she turned her screen toward me. "You found this?" she said without a hello.

That was another thing I liked about my friend—she could get as obsessed with a search as I could. It was a tendency that didn't appeal to everyone, but for me, it was like coming home to sit with someone who could spend hours just scanning archival documents for that one tidbit of information.

"Yep, saw that." She had pulled up Viola's engagement announcement. "Didn't give me much beyond her fiancé's name."

Xzanthia scrolled down. "Did you notice this?" She tapped one long, purple nail on the screen.

I read the sentence she indicated. "McNamara will be attended by Miss Lucy Somerall and Miss Abigail Schuster."

Xzanthia looked at me. "Were you able to locate them?"

I shook my head. "Honestly, I totally missed that part, but you're right. If they were going to be her bridesmaids, they knew her well."

She was already typing before I finished my sentence. "Looks like Somerall has a house here in town. And Schuster, well, she isn't in Octonia, or at least she doesn't own property under her own name here."

I quickly opened my laptop and typed Schuster's name into the genealogy site. Nothing much came up, which was probably a good thing in this case because it meant she was probably still alive. Public records of living individuals were often not available online.

Fortunately, newspapers were, and Xzanthia found Schuster's wedding announcement in our local paper. She'd married a man named Luther Toperman, and another quick search on the GIS site showed they were still local, up in a hollow north of town.

From there, the process of finding contact information was quite quick, and within the hour, each of us had our phones in hand.

I called Somerall, who answered the phone with a cheery "Hello."

"Ms. Somerall, my name is Paisley Sutton. I'm calling about Viola McNamara. Do you have a minute?"

The silence on the other end of the line stretched for quite a long moment before she said, "Yes, dear. I do. What can I do for you?"

I explained that I had found something when salvaging from Ms. McNamara's house and was wondering if I could talk with her about it.

Again, she held a long silence. "I think it might be best if you, Abi, and I talk together."

"Abigail Schu—I mean, Toperman?"

"Yes, dear. I'll call her. Are you free now?"

"Yes, ma'am," I said. "My friend Xzanthia is here, and I believe she's talking to Ms. Toperman. One moment." I put the phone to my chest and caught Xzanthia's eye. "Is she free to meet with us at her place?"

Xzanthia nodded and then, a moment later, asked my question. "Yes, we'll see you there in a half-hour."

I put my phone back to my ear. "Yes, ma'am. We will all meet at Ms. Toperman's place in thirty minutes. Can we bring lunch?"

"Oh, that would be delightful. I'd love a burger," Ms. Somerall said. "See you soon."

Xzanthia quickly took Ms. Toperman's lunch order and then hung up. "Well, this will be interesting," she said.

"It will. Now, does *Lafayette* have what she wants?" I asked, eager to get going.

"Oh yes, they make an excellent tuna salad. But I have no idea why you would order that when you could have one of their burgers."

"Agreed," I said, slipping my laptop back into my bag. "Let's go get lunch and meet some old ladies."

Xzanthia laughed. "Careful, we aren't too much behind them."

She wasn't wrong.

With three of the world's best burgers and a tuna salad sandwich in hand, we drove my car up into the mountains, almost to the end of the public road, and pulled into a gorgeous driveway that led to a farm tucked right against the mountains and the Shenandoah National Park above.

The house looked to be quite old with its assortment of barns and outbuildings, and I couldn't wait to learn more about it if our conversation allowed for such queries. I had to remember that our visit had another purpose, and it wasn't a history lesson, at least not that sort.

When we arrived, two of the most fashionable and stylish women I'd ever seen met us by the car. Between them in their wide-legged pants and flowing blouses with cardigans and Xzanthia in her sleek, pin-striped pants and a collared shirt, I looked downright frumpy, even in one of my best outfits, my good jeans and peasant blouse. Still, the kindness on our hosts' faces eased my nerves about being underprepared.

"I'm Paisley Sutton," I said as I stepped out of the car and extended my hand. The taller and stouter of the two women on the driveway pulled me into a hug that felt both welcoming and strong, while the second woman, a slight but very upright woman, did the same to Xzanthia, who had to bend over quite far to return the greeting.

"It's nice to meet you, Paisley. And you must be Xzanthia Lewis Nicholas," said the woman who had hugged me. "I'm Abigail Toperman, and this is my dearest friend, Lucy Somerall. Please come in."

While I stepped back to the car and grabbed the bags of food, Xzanthia took our drink holder—one just didn't have burgers without a Pepsi in my world—and we followed the two women through a side door into a charming, stone-covered mudroom that led into the most beautiful kitchen I had ever seen. The walls were a warm butter yellow, and the soapstone counters gleamed over the top of creamy white cabinets. A tasteful collection of roosters in various shapes and sizes sat atop the upper cabinets, and on the walls, groupings of paintings, pressed flowers, and different types of tin made the room feel warm and important.

"Let's eat and get to know each other a bit," Ms. Toperman said as she pointed to a round table in the corner of the kitchen.

"This is beautiful," I said to our host. "These windows make this the perfect place for a dining space. Thank you for having us, Ms. Toperman."

"Yes, I love this spot, but please call me Abi. All my friends do," she said.

"Wait until you see the rest of the house," Ms. Somerall said. "The dining room alone is a thing of beauty."

Abi blushed. "You always say that, but to me, this is just home." She smiled as I handed her the tuna salad. "This is perfect."

"Oh, good. I hoped a classic cheeseburger would suit," I said.

"And the the burger with cheese, tomato, lettuce, and red onion, you, Ms. Somerall," Xzanthia said, handing the older woman her burger.

"Lucy, just call me Lucy," she said. "Now, how do you two know each other?"

Xzanthia smiled at me. "We're both history buffs and have worked on a lot of projects together, mostly to help with Paisley's business."

"Oh yes, you're the person who takes the pieces of old houses and helps them find new homes, aren't you?" Abi said. "I love that. I'd save every old home if I could, but since I have my hands full with this one, I'm glad at least some pieces of those homes are saved."

"I feel exactly the same way," I said as I wiped my mouth and grinned. "Some day, I hope to be able to start buying the old places, fixing them up, and then renting them out to families at a reasonable price. We have such a shortage of rentals here." I hadn't really talked about that dream with anyone but Santi, yet somehow, it felt just right to make it more public with these three women.

"Oh, now that is an exciting idea," Lucy said with a wink at Abi. "Maybe we should discuss how we could support that endeavor at another time."

Abi nodded. "Yes, we have other business today, but let's plan to do that. Maybe the four of us could set up a lunch date in town in the near future?"

I looked from Abi to Lucy and nodded. "Yes, please." Then I swallowed hard. "So, as you may have heard, I am the one who found Ms. McNamara's body."

"Yes," Lucy said. "We did hear about that. Poor Viola."

I nodded. "From what I hear, she was a special woman."

Abi smiled. "One of the best this world has ever made. Anyone who had the privilege of knowing her will tell you she was unstoppable."

"Oh yes, her niece Olivia was telling me about her library campaign for Steinem's books," I said, hoping to hear more stories.

Instead, Lucy and Abi frowned.

"You've spoken with Olivia then," Lucy said.

"Yes, I met with her the other day. She wanted a piece of furniture that was going to be demolished in the new owners' renovation, so we picked it up." I studied the women around me and noticed Xzanthia's frown.

"Is there something Paisley should know about Olivia?" she asked.

Lucy and Abi exchanged a look, and then Abi let out a long sigh. "We know she's missing. Not for the first time. The girl disappears for weeks, sometimes months. Made her aunt distraught every time."

I leaned forward. "So she's gone AWOL like this before?"

"A dozen times at least. It started when she was a teenager. Olivia is a nice girl, smart, too, but she's troubled. Her aunt thought maybe she had borderline personality disorder and needed to get professional help. But Olivia's parents doted on her and didn't ever want to confront her about her outbursts or wild decisions. Didn't give the girl much of a chance to succeed," Lucy said.

Well, this was certainly a side of Olivia I hadn't seen in my brief time with her, but then, most people with mental illnesses were very good at masking them, at least for short periods. "Well, that is helpful information. I'll let my husband know."

"She's married to the sheriff," Xzanthia added helpfully. "Good man."

"Oh, yes," Abi said. "We both voted for him. Love to have a Latino man in that role, especially because he's great at it. Need more diversity of all sorts here in Octonia."

I was liking these women more and more every minute. I hoped we could be friends, but I had to get us back to the topic at hand. "When I was salvaging the tiles from Viola's kitchen, I found something."

Abi nodded. "We figured you would when we heard you were hired to do your work there."

These two women were certainly quite well-informed, but then again, it was hard not to be in Octonia.

"So you knew about her hidey-hole?" I said.

Lucy clapped her hands and laughed. "That's exactly what Viola called it. For years, she kept her fun money in that spot alongside the broach and the letter. Said it gave her a little thrill to pull off the tiles and take out some cash for her weekly martini."

I imagined Ms. McNamara all gussied up for a night out and reaching in to take out her "fun money" and smiled. "Oh, I really love that."

Abi nodded. "But I expect you're more interested in hearing about the broach and the note?"

"Yes, ma'am," I said.

Lucy stood. "I'm going to put the kettle on for tea." She stood and walked across the kitchen to an electric kettle, opened the cabinet above, and got out tea bags, a sugar bowl, and a pitcher for cream. Clearly, she was familiar with her friend's kitchen.

"Well, the broach was a gift from Abe. One that Viola treasured. She wore it only once a year, on Christmas itself. She always said she wanted to remember the good times, but I think that broach was just too painful a reminder of what she had lost."

"Her engagement?" Xzanthia asked.

"Yes, and Abe. You know that story?"

"Olivia said they had to break it off because their families didn't support an inter-religious marriage," I said.

"Yes, that was part of it, the biggest part for sure, but as good a man as Abe was, he also didn't really support all that Viola wanted to do. She had big dreams."

Lucy brought a tray with the tea and fixings over to the table. "Viola wanted to start a community center for women down in town, you see." She poured us each a cup. "A place where we could gather to talk, do crafts, and support one another in every way we could."

"Oh, that sounds lovely," I said, thinking I'd like a place like that now. "But Abe didn't like the idea?"

Abi shook her head. "He liked the idea of women getting together to talk and to knit or whatever, but the idea of women helping other women get jobs was just too much ahead of the times for him."

I wondered if JudgeTuskins still felt that way. "So, did he break off the engagement?"

"Actually, no, Viola did," Lucy said as she set a plate of shortbread beside the tea tray. "She said she couldn't be with someone who didn't support all of her dreams. They told everyone it was because of the religious differences, but we knew the real reasons."

"And they cited religion because that would make more sense to people than feminism?" Xzanthia said and then pursed her lips into a tight bow.

"Exactly. It was okay to not marry because of prejudice. But to let on that a woman didn't want to marry a man because he didn't want her empowering other women, that would have been the death knell for Viola's future," Abi said.

"But, and forgive me for saying this," I cleared my throat, "from what Olivia said, Viola was miserable and angry all her life."

Lucy rolled her eyes. "Angry, yes. But in the best way. She was fueled by a desire for equality. She wasn't bitter or resigned, but she made use of the privilege she was given to try to help other women."

"I admire that," I said. "Did I understand correctly that Viola's father and then her brother supported her all her life?"

Lucy and Abigail exchanged another look. "Is that what Olivia said?"

I nodded.

"At first, yes, her father did support her, but Viola was a talented grant writer. She founded a nonprofit that she funded through grants, and as the executive director, she took a small salary that paid all her bills from the time she was twenty-five and on."

"She didn't rely on any man to support her, that's for sure," Lucy added.

I was trying to play catch up mentally, so I said, "And her brother?"

"Oh, he took care of the house," Abi said. "For pay. No handouts—that was Viola's rule."

I nodded and looked at Xzanthia before turning back to the two other women. "So why keep the note and broach from Abe?" I asked.

Lucy leaned forward and took my hand. "Dear, that broach wasn't from Abe."

Chapter Eight

"Apparently, Viola McNamara was very good at keeping secrets," Xzanthia said as we got into the car to begin our drive back to town.

"Apparently," I said. "Those two seemed to know everything about her but not who gave Viola that broach. That seems odd, doesn't it?"

Xzanthia nodded. "Or it's not important."

"What do you mean?" I asked as I drove back onto the larger road toward town.

"It could be just that Viola kept the broach hidden for security reasons," she said. "Just didn't want it lying around or something."

I nodded. That was a possibility I hadn't considered. "But why not put it in a security deposit box or something then."

"Maybe that was an expense she couldn't afford." Xzanthia paused. "But then, if money was tight . . ."

"She could have sold the broach." I sighed. Somehow, this pin was becoming more mysterious all the time.

We arrived back just in time for me to meet Santi at the station for our visit to Abe Tuskins. The judge was expecting us at two, and since Dad and Lucille were picking Sawyer up from school, I was free for the afternoon.

It had been a while since Santi and I had taken a road trip, and although this one was only forty-five minutes long, it was still fun. We put on our favorite playlist—the one from our wedding—and sang along as we drove. Sometimes, the best together times were the ones that didn't require anything more than companionship. I was learning that in this marriage, finally.

When we pulled off a winding road just outside of town and onto a driveway lined with old cedar trees, I knew my afternoon was about to become richer and a lot more complicated. Sure enough, we stopped in front of a large, Federal-style home, and from the wear on the bricks, it looked to be original, not a contemporary construction built in the style. The symmetrical front of the house featured ten windows spaced evenly apart, and the boxwoods out front framed a central doorway.

A small, discreet plaque by the front door noted that the house was built in 1803, and I was dying to look around, in the house but especially out. I had found that my interest in these old plantation houses rarely had anything to do with the owners and far more with the people who had built the structures and kept them running.

"Thomas Jefferson would be proud," Santiago said as he raised the brass knocker on the door.

"He would. Good ole TJ," I said as I thought about our third president and his nearby home, Monticello. Clearly, the owner of this house knew Jefferson—the population at that time would have been too small for two men of means not to be acquainted. "Can we ask for a tour?"

"I wouldn't have started our visit any other way," my husband said as the door swung open and Abe Tuskins greeted us.

"Oh, Ms. Sutton, it's good to see you again," he said as he stretched out his hand. "Sheriff Shifflett said you were coming along. Please come in."

I glanced over at Santi, a bit surprised he had told Tuskins I was coming. "Didn't want him thinking I was hiding something," he whispered as I passed him to follow Tuskins inside.

That made sense, of course. Tuskins was a judge, which meant he had lots of ties to law enforcement. If Santi hadn't disclosed that he knew I'd met Tuskins before, it would be hard for him to seem credible before the Judge

"Judge Tuskins, as you know, Paisley and I are real history buffs. Would it be too much trouble to get a tour?" Santi said as we entered a long central hallway.

Tuskins smiled. "Give you a tour of my pride and joy. . . absolutely. Let's start in here."

We entered a beautiful yellow parlor and then proceeded to follow the judge from room to room as he told us about the pieces of original furniture that had remained with the house for over two hundred years and showed us the portraits of the original owners, a couple with ties to the same agrarian networks as Jefferson and his contemporaries but whose celebrity had faded with time.

When we made our way to the back of the house, we came into a modern kitchen made almost entirely of glass. A large table sat to the left of the kitchen's central island and counters, and Tuskins motioned for us to have a seat as he brought over a pitcher of tea and three glasses.

"Thank you for the tour," I said. "Your house is beautiful."

"Thank you," Tuskins said. "The smaller pieces of history are sometimes overshadowed by the famous ones, but even the little ones are important." He smiled at me. "A fact you well know."

"I do," I said. "Actually, if you wouldn't mind, I'd love to take a walk around the grounds while you and Santi talk. Might that be okay?"

"Of course," he said. "The landscaper was just out, so everything should be prettied up. Good time for a walk."

I smiled at the man and let my hand trail across Santi's back as I made my way to a door just off the kitchen and into the side yard, where a massive white oak stood and shaded the entire west side of the house. "Oh, the tales you could tell, old friend," I said as I put my hand on the trunk. "We say 'if only walls could talk,'" I told my towering companion, "but *I* think the trees probably have the best secrets."

Just then, the wind kicked up, and a branch of the oak swung against the roof of a single-story outbuilding standing just behind it. I walked over to the building and saw from the soot on the ceiling that it was the old summer kitchen. I had some experience with these spaces, and I marveled at the condition of this one. It had wide boards on the floor and ceiling with a loft above and what seemed to be the original loft ladder in one corner. It was beautiful.

Since it wasn't the height of summer—and thus, not the height of snake and heat season—I climbed up the ladder and studied the loft. The space was no more than three feet high, barely high enough to crawl in, yet I knew the enslaved cook had probably slept here.

I shimmied across the space and peered out the small

square window under the table. There, I could see the big house as well as the backyard, where the other workspaces of the plantation would have been.

Off to my right, I saw a gazebo covered in the most amazing wild roses, and I knew I wanted to just sit there for a bit. Once I sat down in the space, which was fragrant with blossoms, I felt some of the tension of the past few days release. The light was dappled, and there was a light breeze. Between the gentle light and the scent of the roses, my body started to relax, and I was soon dozing off. Confident that I'd hear the slap of the screen door when the men came out to find me, I laid down on the bench and made to take a nap.

Instead, my gaze was caught on a tiny brass plaque just up near the base of the rafter above me. I tried to make out what it said from my prone position but gave up, then stood and climbed onto the bench to get a closer look. "For My Viola," it read. Underneath, a sprig of roses was engraved in the metal.

I sat down, wide awake now, and let my brain spin through the possible meanings of this tribute. Clearly, the plaque referred to Viola McNamara—Viola was not a common name in general, but given that Tuskins had once been engaged to her, I didn't feel I was presuming to know it was her.

Since words were how my brain made meaning, I started to talk to myself. "So he dedicated an entire, permanent structure in his yard to her. Planted roses—I wonder if those were her favorites? Did she know about this place? Probably not. It doesn't seem like she and Tuskins had any connection after she broke it off. I'll have to ask Abi and Lucy. I wonder if Tuskins ever married."

I was so deep in my musings that I didn't hear the

screen door or the footfalls approaching me, so I was mid-mumble when Santi and Abe Tuskins stepped into the gazebo. "I see you found my favorite place on the property," Abe said as he sat across from me. "And you clearly noticed the dedication."

I blushed and nodded. "Sorry, I was just thinking about loud."

"Maybe I can help you sort things. Why don't you ask me what you'd like to know?" The old man was smiling, but beneath his kind expression, I could hear the voice of the man who had determined prison sentences for most of his adult life.

I wasn't sure how much the men had heard of my pondering, so I just started at the beginning. "Did Viola like roses?"

"Yes, but not the fancy kind that required a lot of tending. Her favorites were the ones that grow as weeds around here. I upgraded the variety a bit when I had these put in, but they have the same feel." He reached over and caressed a blossom.

"So you loved her all this time," I asked, feeling a surprising emotional tightness in my throat as I spoke.

He nodded. "I did. She broke off our engagement, and I can now see why. But at the time, I was furious. I'm afraid I behaved very poorly. I wish now that I had gotten up the courage to apologize, but I just kept telling myself she didn't want to see me, even for an apology."

I understood. Pride had kept me from apologizing more times than I would have liked in my lifetime. "And you never married?"

"Nope. I didn't want to. I never even dated. Just poured myself into my work and then when I bought this place into keeping it up." He sighed. "I did my best to fill my life well, but it never felt complete."

Regret laced his words, and while I didn't think it likely he'd outwardly express any sadness, it was hard not to feel the weight of his loss in the structure around us. "That's really hard," I said, lost for what else might be appropriate and not dismissive.

"We all have to live with the weight of our choices," the old man said. "Sometimes, we can make good ones, ones that take into account our future, and sometimes, we can't and just have to learn from our mistakes."

I thought for a minute about this insight, about the choices I would have made differently had I known. . . and I knew he was right. Regret was very heavy, but at least we could move forward with a better understanding.

"Well, you have made a beautiful place here, and I love how you've kept the old buildings."

Tuskins looked at the buildings surrounding us and nodded. "All of this history matters," he said.

On our ride home a few minutes later, Santi and I sat quietly for a bit. My brain was weaving around, trying to put threads together. Tuskins was clearly still in love with Viola McNamara, and it seemed that maybe she had still loved him, too, or at least cared for him in some way since she kept his note. Yet they hadn't gotten back to each other, even after all these years and all this societal change, including a shift that would have probably made it possible for her to do all she wanted and for him to approve.

"Unless he still didn't approve?" I blurted out into the car.

"What? Approve of what? Who is he?" Santi glanced over at me. "What are you talking about, baby?" He was laughing now.

I smiled back. "Do you know anything about Judge Tuskins, as a judge, I mean?"

Santi nodded. "I did a little research. He's pretty moderate, it seems. Careful to uphold the letter of the law but also not extreme. Apparently, he has a soft spot for younger people who get into trouble. The attorney I talked to said he likes to give second chances to people who might have made a simple bad choice."

This all aligned with what I'd seen of the man so far—kind but no-nonsense. "So he's not a wild law and order kind of guy, not prone to try to send a message with worse sentences or something?"

My husband chuckled. "You have watched way too many law dramas, Paisley. Yes, judges have predispositions and patterns, but it's not like they can just use the law the way they want."

I sighed. "TV makes everything so much easier."

"Yes, yes, it does," he said. "But what were you thinking that made you ask that?"

I turned in my seat to face him fully. "I'm trying to understand why two people who cared about each other enough to save notes and build gazebos for decades and lived only a little distance apart didn't just get together."

"And you were thinking Tuskins might have still been a bit anti-feminist?"

"You know me so well. Did you get any sense of that?"

Santi shook his head. "No, but I will say that in this job, I find people are not always consistent. In fact, we rarely are. He could be pretty open-minded about some things but still thinks women shouldn't work. You know what I mean?"

I did know. My own dad was that way—totally great with my friends' trans kids but still thought homeless people should just get a job. Some belief systems were just further entrenched than others.

I sighed and turned back to rest against my seat as my brain continued to pick through the tidbits of information we'd learned in the past week. Olivia Weiss had a history of disappearing, a fact Santi had found rather infuriating since no one had told him that when he started looking for her. The hidden broach with the note from Abe Tuskins wasn't from Abe Tuskins. And now, Tuskins had built a rose-covered shrine of sorts to his lost love but had not, in fact, ever gone back to try to make things right, at least that we knew of.

"I can hear you thinking," Santi said. "Want to spill it all out and see what you find?"

Goodness, he knew me well. I closed my eyes and started to talk. "Two people in love for almost sixty years and living just miles apart never get back together. The woman's niece believes—or at least wants us to believe—that her aunt hated Tuskins, but then, it turns out that the niece isn't best known for the truth, or Viola's two best friends are lying, and Olivia is telling the truth. And that pin isn't from Viola's long-lost love, but it's worth $25,000. She only wore it once a year, but it wasn't a secret, despite the fact it was tucked behind the tiles in her kitchen." I paused to take a breath.

"So, it seems like we need to figure out who is credible —Olivia or Abi and Lucy. Then, we need to see if we can find out who gave Viola that broach. Or maybe she bought it herself. I hadn't thought of that before." I looked over at Santi.

He shrugged. "Her bank account doesn't show any kind

of big purchase like that—she's banked in town for the past fifty-eight years. But the pin might not have been that expensive when she bought it."

"I think Cartier has always been Cartier," I said.

"So then, maybe she saved cash and bought it that way?"

I sighed. "Could be, I guess. But if you bought yourself something expensive, something that you could use pretty often, would you only take it out once and then hide it in a secret location when you weren't using it?" Something about that didn't add up.

"Good point. When Sawyer and I get our McLaren, we'll be taking that out every day after school." Santi laughed. He and my son had the same dream car, a $300,000 dream car, and so far, Sawyer had saved up $32.17 to buy it.

"Keep saving those pennies, love," I said. "But yeah, that's what I mean. If you buy something nice for yourself, you usually want to show it off, right?"

"Right, but if you don't want people to ask a lot of questions about where you got something. . ."

"I think that broach is where I look next." I smiled at him. "If that's okay with the sheriff."

"If it wasn't, would you stop?" he said with a small smile.

"No, but I'd tell you what I was doing. I don't do secrets, remember?"

"Fair enough. Tell me what you find?"

"Of course. I always tell you everything." I leaned back in the seat, took out my phone, and searched for local jewelers. Maybe they'd have a lead.

I made two appointments with jewelers in Charlottesville, the nearest big city, for the next day, but for tonight, Sawyer was home and hungry. It amazed me how much a tiny human could eat, but he consumed two tubes of yogurt, a clump of grapes, two prosciutto and mozzarella wraps, and a large bowl of popcorn—before dinner. It was as if his entire body was a stomach. I was going to have to up my food budget when he became a teenager.

Still, he was in great spirits, so while I sat in a chair with Jade curled up by my feet and let the spring breeze waft over me, he climbed his treehouse and conducted an imaginary battle with the invading troll forces. Apparently, his main weapon was rotten apples launched by a trebuchet, and I had to wonder for a moment when he had learned what a trebuchet was. I supposed most parents had this sort of "Wow, I didn't know he knew that" moment, but because he spent weekends away from me, I had the almost constant experience of him learning new things without me.

For instance, he wanted a bottle of Stewart's root beer the other day. Since I was trying hard to toe the line about not making any foods bad and, therefore, more desirable, I gave in because it didn't have caffeine. And then, when we got outside, he couldn't get the top off. Before I could intervene, he took the bottle, pounded the cap against a bridge window ledge, and popped off the top. Obviously, his father had been teaching him new things.

Still, I figured this experience would help prepare me for when he left home. I hoped that maybe I wouldn't be as devastated as I imagined I would be. Now, though, just the thought made me feel like someone was trying to remove my heart from my chest.

"Sawyer," I said, "where did you learn about the trebuchet?"

"In school. Ms. Ross is teaching us about the middle-evil period," he said as he pretended to load another bushel of rotten fruit on his imaginary machine.

"Ah, yes, the middle-evil period. What else have you learned about it?" I asked after he had completed his launch sequence.

"When people got married then, they were really stinky, so that's why they carried flowers." He spouted off this random fact with aplomb, and I remembered when I had learned the same thing much later in high school when studying Chaucer.

"Oh yes, well, there's that," I said, laughing.

He walked to the edge of the treehouse and leaned over the railing. "She had a piece of jewelry from way back then," he said. "A hair thing. It was real gold and very heavy."

I stared at my son. "Ms. Ross brought a medieval-era gold hairpiece to your class?"

"Yep, we got to pass it around very carefully." His face was very serious. "She had a picture of a knight, too. They didn't find dinosaurs, though. Dinosaurs are older."

I smiled at his beautiful sense of history. "What did you learn about knights?"

"They wore all this metal armor to protect themselves, and when someone wanted to marry them, they gave them a hand-cher-chef."

"Ah yes, the famous tribute," I said. "You are learning a lot." It was a little odd that his teacher was investing time in the medieval period with kids this young, but then again, he was learning, so what did I care?

I put my head back to look up at the clouds whizzing by and then closed my eyes. The image of a gold clip floated into my mind as I tried to imagine what Sawyer had seen today. Then I thought about taking one of my old T-shirts and giving it to Santi as a joke—my tribute. If I had given him one of the ones with huge holes in it before we got married, he might have had a little bit clearer picture of exactly who he was marrying. I never threw a still wearable piece of clothing away, no matter how many holes it had.

A thought zinged through my mind, and I sat up straight. Viola's pin. What if it wasn't something someone had given to her but something she had been going to give to someone else? Not a man, though. Even now, most men I knew wouldn't wear a broach, especially one that big. No, she would have wanted to give it to a woman.

What woman? A lover? A good friend? Her mother? I realized I hadn't heard anything about her mother, which was curious. And according to everything Xzanthia had found, Viola's sister, Victoria, had died years ago. Didn't have any sisters. While I couldn't discount that Viola may have been in love with another woman, I hadn't seen anything to indicate that she was a lesbian. Maybe it was intended for Abi or Lucy? But then why tell them about it and not give it to them? Would one of them have been jealous of the other?

I had no proof at all that this broach was supposed to be a gift from Viola, but somehow, that possibility felt more plausible than that it was given to her by someone and only brought out on special occasions. It was obviously very important to her, but it was also clearly something she didn't want to see on a daily basis or even bring out more than once a year. That seemed to indicate she had some conflicted feelings about it.

Sawyer, having finished with this apple assault on the trolls, was again hungry, so the two of us made our way up the hill to the house to begin dinner. While Saw fed Jade, I prepped the jar of spaghetti sauce with extra spices and some sliced mushrooms and pondered how exactly I could find out more about the broach. Did Cartier keep a record of who owned their pieces? That felt like something I'd need to ask the Antiques Roadshow about, and while I didn't have any access to the experts on either the British or American versions of the show, I did have one possible source who might just be able to shed some light on the mystery of the Christmas tree.

The next morning, before my first jeweler's appointment, I made my way up to the tiny town of Aroda and parked in front of what used to be the community's local market but was now a hub for antiques, especially antique jewelry. Roo Sullivan owned the place, and she knew more about costume jewelry than anyone I'd ever met. I hadn't really thought about coming to see her before because she specifically did not deal with precious metals or stones. Still, I was confident she'd be able to tell me something about Viola's broach.

Roo was a long-limbed, big-haired white woman who wore almost as much jewelry as she sold. When I entered her store, she was sporting a purple jumpsuit and matching purple earrings, rings, and necklace. Roo was not a person who felt there was such a thing as "too much of a good thing."

"Paisley Sutton, as I live and breathe," she said in her affected nearly Texan accent. "Find some more costume jewelry to sell me?"

I had gotten to know Roo because a few of the salvage jobs I'd done had included the contents of the houses themselves, so she was now my go-to person for any jewelry I found there. She always bought the good costume stuff, was happy to give me advice about how to price the stuff she didn't want to sell, and had told me on more than one occasion when something I thought was fake was actually the real deal. She'd earned my trust, and I was betting she'd have good information for me now, too.

"I did find some jewelry," I said as I took out my phone, "but it's not costume or, at least, not entirely." I opened the photo of the broach and set it on the counter. "I'm hoping you might be able to tell me something about this pin."

Roo let out a long, slow wolf whistle. "A Cartier Christmas tree, holy cow. This is worth a mint, you know?"

"I do know," I said. "Can you tell me a bit about it?"

She shook her head. "I don't know much since this kind of piece isn't my specialty, as you know." She took a deep breath. "But it is twenty-four-karat gold. Those are real rubies and emeralds, and even the paste stones are high quality."

"But you don't know anything?" I teased. "Any idea if anywhere local would have sold it back in the day?"

"Like when it was new?" she looked at me incredulously. "So, this isn't one of your typical queries, huh?"

I shook my head. "I found this in the McNamara house."

Roo put the back of her hand to her forehead. "Oh Lord, in the dead woman's house. Was this hers?"

I nodded. "She had it for decades, or so her friends said."

She leaned down and looked at the picture again. "Yeah, it's from the 50s. I can get you the exact year if you want to wait a minute."

"Please," I said, and she skedaddled back to her work-room, where she kept her computer.

The age of the piece had been one of the questions I was going to ask the jeweler, but if I could learn it now, all the better. I might just be able to skip the trip to Char-lottesville after all.

Roo was back in less than two minutes and said, "It was a limited edition piece in 1954. Only 200 were made, which makes the thing even more valuable than I had thought."

I was pretty sure we'd estimated the value correctly, but double-checking my facts had never harmed me.

"It went for $47,552 at an auction in New York last month," she said.

I braced myself against the glass case in front of me. "Forty-seven thousand. Dollars?"

"Yes, American dollars. The gold alone is worth a fortune, but add in the gems and the rarity of the piece. Oh, and the fact that it is Cartier. . . well, it's one of the most expensive mass-produced pieces I've ever seen."

"If you consider 200 copies mass-produced," I said as I stared at my phone.

"Fair point. I expect each of these would have been made from a mold," she said. "But the stones would have been laid by hand." She picked up my phone. "If I could see the piece, I could tell you more."

I looked up at her. "You free now?"

Roo didn't hesitate and grabbed her huge purple purse. "No one will miss me," she said as she came around the counter. "Where are we going?"

"The pin is in evidence."

"Ooh, an adventure to the police department. This just keeps getting better." She put her hand under her hair and puffed it up—as if it needed it.

I shot Santi a quick text before we headed back toward town, and when we got to the sheriff's office, he was waiting in an interview room with the broach on a white napkin. "We spare no expense for the good stuff," he said as he pointed at the napkin. "Feels a little cheap, huh?"

"You have no idea," I said as Roo went immediately to the broach and whistled again.

"May I?" she said as she moved to pick up the pin.

Santi nodded. "Sure." He looked at me carefully. "What's up?"

"Just give her a quick minute," I said.

Roo set the pin in her palm and bounced her hand just a little. Then she reached into her bag, pulled out a jeweler's scope, and brought it to her face.

When she sat down hard in the chair behind her, I spat out my breath. "What is it, Roo?"

"Those aren't paste, Paisley. This thing is entirely, one hundred percent real stones."

Chapter Nine

After asking Roo to keep her discovery quiet, Santi and I gave her a lift back to her shop, then drove down to keep my appointment at the jeweler in Charlottesville. Roo had assured us he was reputable and discreet, and we now needed a full evaluation of the broach. If it had been a motive for murder before, it now provided an even bigger motive if it was encrusted with diamonds.

As we headed down 29 toward town, Santi said, "So, this thing could be worth, what, a hundred K?"

I shook my head as I flicked through images and prices for other Cartier broaches. "I have no idea, but if it's a one-of-a-kind Cartier, probably more. There's one in here for $155,000." The piece was about the same size and was a panther covered completely in diamonds. "But it's got fewer karats of diamonds if Roo's estimate was right." I looked at the listing on the actual Cartier site, "and this one is new, I think. So. . ."

"So if this one is vintage, it's probably worth more," Santi finished.

"Exactly," I said. "Do you think Viola knew what she had?"

Santi sighed. "I have no idea. It's hard for me to imagine someone putting something that valuable in the wall, but then, my mom still doesn't have a bank account because she doesn't trust them. People make strange choices when it comes to money."

I put my head against the window and watched the strip malls and car dealerships fly by as we headed downtown. I knew we were missing something, but I just couldn't figure it out. It felt like there had to be a connection between this pin and Viola's death, but it was absolutely possible this was all a coincidence. That Viola had died for some reason other than the broach.

Santi found us a free parking space near the courthouse, and we walked the few blocks to the Downtown Mall and up to the jewelry store on the corner. The shop was small but beautiful, with navy blue velvet in the bottom of all the jewelry cases and a sparkling collection of pieces displayed attractively. From the research I had done online, this shop was the most elite in the area. It catered to a very specific clientele.

I, however, was not looking very elite in my yoga pants, tennis shoes, and T-shirt, but my hope was that Santi's uniform made up for my casualness. When a small, bespectacled man came out to greet us, he immediately smiled and said, "You must be Ms. Sutton and Sheriff Shifflett."

"Yes. Thank you for seeing us," I said.

"Of course. Let's take this into the back. My assistant will tend the shop," he said.

A middle-aged woman with a sleek haircut and pleasant smile stepped from behind a nearby counter and nodded.

The three of us filed into a small, well-lit room with a

central counter and an array of what looked like micro-scopes. "May I see the piece?" our host asked.

"Of course," I said, unwrapping it from the red and white bandana I'd used in place of Santi's napkin. Still, even with the upgrade, it felt a little lame to have a very pricey piece of jewelry stuffed into the side pocket of my purse, even in the bandana.

The jeweler put on white gloves and then carefully picked up the pin. He turned it over, slipped in a jeweler's loop, and held the piece under a bright light.

"Definitely authentic Cartier," he said. "And twenty-four-karat gold certainly." He pulled the piece closer and then looked at each of the stones. "And each of these stones is authentic and of the highest clarity and color."

He set the piece down and looked at us. "This is one of the few Christmas-themed pieces Cartier has ever made." He smiled. "You have an extremely valuable piece here. If you don't mind waiting"—he gestured to two chairs at the edge of the room—"I'll write up the appraisal for you."

We nodded and sat down to watch him weigh, measure, and study the piece some more. After a few minutes, he finally took out a triplicate document and began to write. Then, when he handed us the top copy of the form, I almost dropped it.

I cleared my throat. "Does that say $234,000?"

Santi took the paper from my hands and then looked at the jeweler. "Really?"

"As I said, the piece is very valuable." He smiled at us. "If the owner should ever wish to sell, I would be honored to broker the exchange."

He then spent a few minutes giving us the weight of the diamonds, their value, and the weight and value of the rubies and emeralds, too. We had a full appraisal document and a healthy amount of shock when we left.

It was my turn to wolf whistle as we walked up the mall. "We should get this back to the sheriff's office," I said.

"In a minute. First, dumplings," Santi said. "I know how you love them."

He wasn't wrong, and normally, I wouldn't hesitate to have a double portion of Marco and Luca's amazing pork dumplings, but knowing how much this broach was worth made me nervous. "It's okay."

"Pais, you're with a police officer. We can get dumplings to go." He put his arm around my waist and led me further up the mall toward the dumpling shop.

As he ordered, I stood close by with my purse conspicuously pulled to my chest. I felt like a tourist who was too overzealous about guarding their passport, but I couldn't help it. A quarter of a million dollars was in my bag, wrapped in the scarf I'd had on my hair the day before.

We got dumplings, sesame noodles, and sodas, and I was already halfway into mine before Santi even got the car out of the space. These things were so good, and their tastiness, combined with the relief I felt at not having been mugged for the broach, made me famished.

However, I did manage to stop stuffing my face long enough to shovel dumplings and some noodles into Santi's mouth as he drove. By the time we were headed back north, both of us had full bellies and a lot of questions.

"So, a quarter of a million-dollar pin is shoved into a wall above the kitchen sink?" I said. "Have you ever seen anything like that?"

"Never," he said. "I've found caches of money, savings bonds, and even jewelry, but nothing like this."

I glanced at my watch and saw it was a little before one. "Want to meet my new friends?" I said. "I think we have enough time to get there and back before I have to get Sawyer off the bus."

"Get where?"

I smiled and picked up my phone.

Abigail answered on the first ring, and within five minutes, we had her assurances that she'd call Lucy and meet us in a half-hour. When she asked what it was about, I just mumbled something about Viola and the broach. I figured there was no need to give away more information than necessary.

As we drove past Octonia and up into the mountains, Santi's cell phone rang, and when he answered, his face immediately fell. "Can you handle the scene for a couple of hours? I need to make one stop before I come down."

When he hung up, I watched his face carefully. "Crime scene?"

He nodded. "Murder scene. We found Olivia McNamara."

My heart kicked against my chest. "She's dead."

"Drowned, apparently. Just up the road here." He pointed across a small bridge that we were just passing. "Looks like it happened a couple of days ago."

I twisted in my seat as we passed the bridge over the Rolling River running beside the road. "What was she doing up here?" I asked, almost to myself.

"I don't know, but we are going to find out." He gunned the engine. "I'll need you to let me take the lead now, Paisley."

"Of course," I said and took a deep breath. Our

friendly chat had just taken a much more serious turn. Even so, I couldn't help but think that Sawyer would be thrilled that Jade was most likely going to become a permanent addition to our family.

When we pulled into Abi's driveway, Santi turned on the lights and squawked the siren briefly as his way, I suppose, of letting them know this was official police business. As he stepped out of the car, he said, "Bring the broach, but don't show it to them."

I studied him as he marched toward the front door, and then I followed a few steps behind. I'd seen my husband interrogate people before, and while he was never violent or even loud, there was a certain energy he exuded during these tougher moments of his job that was both intriguing and, frankly, terrifying. I did not think Abi and Lucy were going to like these next few minutes very much at all.

Santi rapped hard on the door near the kitchen, and when Abi opened the door, he said, "Ms. Toperman, Sheriff Santiago Shifflett. I need to ask you a few questions."

Abi's eyes flew to me, but I just looked back at her. She wasn't going to get my comfort in the face of my husband's questions.

"Yes. Please, come in," she said and held open the door for us.

I had tucked the broach into the phone pocket of my yoga pants, where it bulged, but I was hoping that the women would think it was keys or something under my baggy shirt. If Santiago didn't want them to see it, he had a reason.

Lucy was sitting at the kitchen table when we walked in, but as soon as she saw Santi's expression, she stood up. "Oh my, what is wrong?"

Santi motioned for her to sit back down and pulled out a chair so Abigail could, too. He then let me step in front of him to take another seat before he pulled a chair around to the head of the table and sat down himself. "The body of Olivia McNamara was just found up the road by the old Quaker camp."

"Oh my," Lucy said as her hands flew to her mouth. "That poor girl."

I looked from her to Abi, who was sitting, lips apart, staring.

"It appears she drowned," Santi continued. "Have either of you had any contact with her in the past few days?"

The women looked at each other and then shook their heads. "No, none," Abi said. "Paisley here told us she was missing, but we haven't seen her." She twisted her fingers together. "Who would have done something like this?"

"That's what we will figure out," Santi said. "Do you know anyone who might have wanted to hurt her?" His tone was still all business.

The two women again exchanged a glance, but neither said anything. "No, not anyone," Lucy finally said.

Santi stood. "I have to make a phone call and check in at the scene. I'll be right back." As he turned away from the table, he shot me a wink. Fortunately, I knew that signal and gave him a crisp nod.

As soon as the door shut behind him, I said, "I'm sorry about that. When he gets a serious case like this, he has to be all business."

"Of course, dear," Abi said as the tension in the room eased. "Does he have any leads?"

I shook my head. "Not that I know of. He doesn't tell me much about his cases. I just can't imagine who would have wanted to hurt poor Olivia. I mean, from what you said, she wasn't the most reliable person, but being flaky doesn't usually warrant murder."

I was playing up my confusion just a bit since I wanted to act the part Santi needed. But I was also very confused. Who would want to kill a young woman? Who would want to kill an old woman, for that matter?

Lucy cleared her throat. "We may have, um, not told you the whole story about Olivia on your last visit."

Abi sighed. "We try not to gossip, you see," she said.

Inwardly, I rolled my eyes, but to them, I said, "I totally understand. Is there something else we should know?" I wasn't going to pretend I wouldn't immediately repeat what they said to Santi, but I also knew they were dying to do just what they said they didn't want to do—gossip.

"Well, Olivia ran with kind of a bad crowd," Lucy said. "They rode motorcycles and had those discs in their ears."

"And the tattoos," Abi said as she threw a hand in the air.

I felt a little mental whiplash at this very conservative perspective on tattoos and gauges from these women who had made it seem like they were the pinnacle of feminist virtue on my last visit.

"Don't get us wrong. People can dress how they'd like and ride those death traps if they want, but this group was just"—Lucy cleared her throat again—"pardon my French, despicable."

I stifled a chuckle at the fact that Lucy would feel the need to ask for grace when using the word *despicable* and simply nodded. I wasn't sure I could hold my tongue about this level of prejudice if I spoke, and I needed these women to keep talking.

"We thought they'd grow out of it when they reached

adulthood, but if anything, they seemed to get worse. Their whole bodies were covered in pictures, pictures that would get wrinkly and saggy as they got older," Abi added.

"We tried to explain this to Olivia, but she wouldn't hear of it," Lucy said and then literally tsk-tsked.

I took a deep breath and asked the question at the forefront of my mind. "And what did Viola, her aunt, think of Olivia and her friends?"

Lucy sighed. "She just said there were worse things than green hair and tattoos."

I forced back my smile. At least Viola was a woman with a truly open mind.

"I see," I said. "Did Olivia have lots of tattoos, too? I saw her gauges—the discs in her ears," I added, "but I didn't see many tattoos."

Abi rolled her eyes. "The young woman thought she was going to be an actress, so she kept her 'body art,' as she called it, under her clothes. At least she had that much common sense."

"But you didn't think she had much chance of becoming an actor?" I said.

"*Actress*, dear," Lucy said. "It's the feminine form of the word."

I bit my tongue to keep from explaining gender-neutral language and how the twenty-first century strode toward equality and simply asked my question in a new way. "Did she ever have any acting parts?"

Abi nodded. "She got the lead in the Four County Players a couple of times, but always in those new plays, not any of the classics."

I allowed my jaw to clench for just a minute as the prejudices of my new acquaintances grew by the minute. "Well, the Players are a pretty serious company. That's impressive. Did she want to act on stage?"

"No, dear," Lucy said. "She thought she was Hollywood-bound. Said she had a lead on a show with that Hawaiian-looking guy."

"Oh, that's right," Abi said as she looked at me. "You know the one who talks like he's stupid?"

I winced and then said, "Keanu Reeves. She had a potential role with Keanu Reeves?"

"That's what she said," Lucy said. "But as I told you, she was always a bit free with the truth."

I was at a total loss now because if these two women were truthful, Olivia was not. But then, maybe they were just close-minded enough not to really want to see the truth. "Did she tell you the name of the movie?" Maybe I could track down more information if I had a bit more details.

Lucy looked at Abigail. "It was some sequel. The third one or something. I didn't really pay attention because she couldn't be trusted and because, well, we all know sequels are terrible."

I couldn't dispute the sequels thing, but Keanu Reeves was one of my favorite celebrities if he wasn't the best actor. "John Wick?"

Abi tapped her nose like we were playing charades. "That's it. I remember because I thought it was probably about candles."

I didn't dare disillusion this woman with her sweet but naïve vision and tell her about the extremely violent action films. "That would have been a big role," I said, hoping to help these women see that, at the very least, Olivia was aiming high with her stories.

"She tried to get us to watch one of those late-night shows, but I have a strict no TV after the late news policy,"

Abi said. "She said she'd send us a link to see it on the computer, but I don't trust those link things."

"Wait, she was on a late-night talk show?" I said as my heart rate kicked up. "Do you have that link?"

"Of course," Abi said. "I keep all my emails filed by the name of the person who sent them, just in case." She studied my face and then said, "Would you like to see it?"

"Yes, please," I said.

Abigail led me over to a computer so ancient I was surprised it could go online, but just a split second later, her AOL account popped up, and she navigated to a folder with Olivia's name on it. In the last email that Olivia sent was information about Jimmy Fallon and a link.

"May I?" I said as I resisted the urge to push Abi out of the way to get to the keyboard myself.

"Of course, dear," she said, letting me take her chair.

I clicked on the link, and it sent me to YouTube, where I proceeded to see a clip of Olivia from Octonia on the couch with Keanu Reeves, talking to Fallon about the latest John Wick movie in which Olivia played the love interest. After the clip played, I sat there, stunned.

Abi and Lucy watched as well, but the significance of Olivia's accomplishment was obviously lost on them because all they could talk about was how Reeves needed a haircut and a shave.

Still, this was big news—it meant Olivia had a successful acting career with a major studio. She wasn't some wannabe. She had made it.

It didn't seem worth it trying to dispel these two women of what they believed. They had clearly decided who Olivia was, and sharing a couch with Keanu wouldn't change that.

Santi had not yet returned from his phone call, and I was beginning to wonder if something worse had happened. "Well, ladies, thank you for your time. I better be going since Santi has a crime scene to get to."

Lucy fluttered her hands again. "That poor girl," she said. "Why would anyone want to kill her?"

"That's a good question," I said as we walked toward the door. "If you think of anything Santi should know, you'll be in touch with him, right?"

"Absolutely," Abi said as she stood by the door. "And you'll keep us posted on services when you hear?"

"Of course," I said as I glanced over above the stove. "What a beautiful collection of cast-iron skillets. Do you use those?"

Abi turned a deep shade of scarlet but said casually, "Of course. They were my mother's. My pride and joy," she added.

"I love cooking with cast iron, but I'm afraid I don't take very good care of mine. I'm too reliant on my nonstick stuff that can go in the dishwasher."

Abi opened the door and put her hand on my back to usher me out. Clearly, she was not interested in talking about housekeeping. "Thank you for coming by," she said, waving at Santi before quickly closing the door, almost in my face.

I stood and stared at the blue wooden door for a long minute and then turned to Santi, who was holding the phone to his ear but had eyes only for me. He was faking.

"So, what did you learn?" he said as he got into the car beside me.

I recounted what the women had said about Olivia and her acting "aspirations" and then told him about the Fallon clip.

"Wow," he said. "So she was doing just fine, probably financially, too?"

"I'd say so. I mean, it wasn't going to set her up for life or anything, but I imagine she was financially quite solvent." I studied the road as we drove. "So that takes away one motive for murder. She didn't need the broach to pay her bills."

Santi bounced his head back and forth. "Well, not necessarily. While you might be satisfied with enough money, some people always want more."

I sighed. "Right. That's true. But do we really think she might have killed her aunt?"

"I doubt it. Didn't those women tell you Olivia disappeared for periods, and no one knew where she was?"

"They did," I said, sitting up straighter in my seat. "But she was probably just away shooting."

"That's what I'm thinking. I think our energy might be better spent on figuring out why two old women want to discredit a young woman who was their best friend's niece."

When we arrived at the bridge a few minutes later, Santi suggested I drive his cruiser back to town. "I'll be here a while, and then I can just ride back with Forest." He kissed my cheek. "And I'll tell you everything when I get home."

I couldn't beat that offer. I didn't have to stand out in the chilly afternoon, stressing about whether or not I'd be home in time to get Sawyer off the bus, *and* I wasn't going to miss out on anything. "Deal," I said and walked around the car.

As I drove home, I reviewed my conversation with Lucy and Abigail. They obviously did not like Olivia McNamara, and while they made it sound like it was just because they had a poor opinion of her and her friends, I sensed there was something more behind their words.

I'd have to ponder how to suss that out, but for now, I wanted to look into Olivia's acting career. It was possible she had landed the role as Reeves's leading woman as her first role, but that seemed unlikely. So, as soon as I got home, I pulled out my laptop and googled Olivia's name.

Sure enough, the woman had been in numerous films and had even played a minor character in a *Law and Order: SVU* episode a few years back. It seemed she was a rising star, which made it even odder that Abigail and Lucy hadn't wanted to brag about her. My friends' kids were like my own when it came to singing their praise for everything from straight As to a great lacrosse game. Why wouldn't they want to cheer her on in her career?

Still, I did know people whose prejudices ran deep. A parent of one of Sawyer's closest friends once told my son that people who had tattoos were "dirtbags," a fact that we had to counter quickly, especially since Santi had several. Some people thought their opinions justified them to say anything.

Now, I was at the difficult point of trying to decide if I could trust anything that Abigail and Lucy had said. I knew I would have to fill Santi in on things, too, but for now, I was simply musing on my own. Well, mostly. I did call Mika because it had occurred to me that she might know some of these tattooed and pierced friends of Olivia's who put Abi and Lucy off so much. She ran with a much cooler group than I did in high school, and while she wasn't an Octonia native like I was, she did socialize far more than I did.

When I called, she was ringing up a customer, so I waited a few minutes, then gave her the rundown about Olivia's acting career and what Lucy and Abigail had said about her friends. "Do you know who any of those people might be?"

"So you called me to see if I knew who the freaks might be? Is that what you're saying?" Mika asked with a laugh.

"I did not use the word *freaks*," I replied sharply. "Sorry. I'm a little on edge after my conversation this morning."

"No wonder. It's always difficult to feel at ease when you aren't sure what the truth is." She took a deep breath. "Okay, so I do know a couple of people who ride motorcycles in town. One is this guy, Devon, who also knits. He's huge, wins weight-lifting competitions, and has lots of tattoos."

"Sounds like the kind of person who would put Abi and Lucy way off. Do you have contact information for him?"

Mika snorted. "Believe it or not, he's due here this afternoon. He always comes in on Tuesdays and knits with me for a bit."

"Oh, what time?" Sawyer was due off the bus in thirty minutes, but maybe I could bring him along.

"Comes in before his shift as a bouncer at some club downtown, so probably about five," she said. "Bring pizza and the kid. We'll teach him how to knit."

I loved my best friend. She knew me so well. "Oh, can I learn, too?"

"Yes, Paisley, I will once again attempt to teach you to knit so that you can promptly forget everything because you don't practice. And then I'll teach you again. This cycle is simply part of our friendship now."

I laughed as I hung up. Now, I just had to figure out a way to talk to Devon without giving away more than I should about the murder investigations.

I shouldn't have worried because my young son had a million questions that he was not too shy to ask as soon he saw a huge black man with lots of tattoos and piercings. To his credit, Devon seemed completely unfazed and told Sawyer the story of each tattoo and explained why he liked body ornamentation so much.

"It's kind of like clothes you wear," he said. "But you don't have to change them. You just pick something you really love, and then you get to keep it on forever." Devon smiled at my son. "*But* you need to wait a few years before you start getting piercings or tattoos, okay?"

Saw frowned. "But I'm half a grown-up. I can do what I want. My body, my rules."

Devon chuckled. "That's so true, but your body is still growing, so if you got a tattoo right now, it would stretch out. Your Sonic the Hedgehog might end up looking like a big, blue blob, and who wants a tattoo of a big blue blob?"

Sawyer nodded, "Maybe when I'm eight."

I laughed. "Let's try eighteen," I said as Mika once again took my knitting needles from me and showed me how to cast on. I was hopeless.

"She's right, Sawyer," Devon said as he carefully checked the dishcloth that my son was almost finished knitting. "Most tattoo artists won't tattoo anyone under eighteen."

"Mom, how long until I'm eighteen?" Sawyer asked.

"Eighty-five years," I said, and all the grown-ups chuckled. Sawyer nodded as if I had said six months and kept knitting like a pro.

The ice broken by the kiddo, I told Devon that I was curious if he'd known Olivia McNamara.

Devon's face opened in a wide smile. "Oh yeah, Liv and

I are tight. When she's here, I mean. That Hollywood stuff has her gone a lot."

So he knew she was an actor. That was the first question answered. "Yeah, I saw her interview with Keanu Reeves and Jimmy Fallon. She was so funny."

"That's Liv," he said. "She is a tiny parcel of wit and vigor."

Mika cleared her throat and looked at me with a fierce stare, the universal communication for "Say something."

"Devon, I'm really sorry to have to be the one to tell you this, but Olivia's body was found this afternoon." My voice squeaked a little as I spoke.

Sawyer looked from me to Devon and then back to me. "She died, Mom?"

I looked at him. "Yes, love bug, she did." I had never balked at telling Sawyer about death, and while we didn't dwell on the subject, I figured it didn't do any good to hide its existence from him. That said, I wasn't going to tell him the woman had been murdered. Death was natural; murder was the opposite.

"Sawyer, I have some chocolate milk in the back. Want to help me get everyone a glass?"

My son hopped up, and as he followed Mika to the back, I finally met Devon's eyes. "I'm so sorry."

The sock he was knitting floated halfway between his legs and his shoulders as he looked at me. "What happened?"

"Well, actually, she was murdered. I was hoping you might have some idea why," I said.

He leaned forward and whispered, "Liv was murdered? Everyone loved her. She was the belle of Octonia."

I thought, *Well, not everyone*, but I didn't say anything. "So you can't think of anyone who might want to hurt her?"

Devon put his sock in his lap and shook his head. "Not a single person. She really kind of kept to herself. A few of us hung out sometimes, friends from high school who had kept in touch. But she spent so much time away these days, we didn't see each other often."

"If you or your friends think of anything that might be relevant, could you call the sheriff? He's my husband," I said.

Devon nodded sternly and then slipped his knitting and yarn into a bright green grocery bag. "Will you tell Paisley and Sawyer good night for me?"

"Of course," I said and watched him leave. I was sad to be the bearer of such bad news, but I would rather have him hear it from me in this safe place than hear it tonight when he needed to create a safe space. He had looked devastated.

As the bell over Mika's front door chimed, Sawyer and she returned to the front of the shop. "Oh, did Devon leave?" she asked.

"Yes, he said to tell you two goodbye. He had to go take care of some things." I kept my voice light, but I held Mika's gaze to let her know that it was more than just errands that had led Devon to depart early.

"He must be sad," Sawyer said. "I'd be sad if my friend died."

I pulled my little man into my hip and said, "Yeah, me, too, Saw. I think Devon is sad."

"I'm going to give him my dishcloth," he said. "Maybe that will make him feel better."

Mika smiled. "I think so, Sawyer. Now, let me show you how to cast off?"

A half-hour later at home, we had the pizza we'd forgotten to eat with Mika as our lukewarm supper, and Sawyer showed Santi his bright blue dishcloth. "I'm going to give it to my friend Devon because he's sad."

Santi ruffled the kid's hair and admired the dishcloth with genuine enthusiasm. He had witnessed enough of my failed knitting attempts to know that the child had surpassed his mother.

"Brush teeth and put on pj's, Saw. It's bedtime," I said.

"Okay, Mom," he said. "Then videos."

"Yep, Buddy. Then videos before a story," I replied.

As soon as he was out of the room, Santi said, "Then, something mindless and some cross-stitch for you." His face was firm. "You need to slow down your brain for a bit."

He was right. My mind felt like it was spinning from possibility to possibility, and I couldn't land on anything useful when I was like this. "Excellent, I have a new pattern to start."

Santi smiled. He knew I was a completer, someone who finished everything she started—books she hated, shows she got bored with, and cross-stitch projects that had lost their excitement. So, the chance to start something new was a big deal.

"I'll take bedtime. You go ahead and get going."

I smiled, went to hug Sawyer good night, and then sat down with my new pattern. As usual, I'd picked it out from Etsy, and it showed a great white shark nestled among coral. The entire pattern included only twenty-six colors, and while there were a lot of stitches, it was something I could work easily and then hang in Sawyer's room. The boy was obsessed with these fish.

I opened my antique sewing stand, a lucky find at an estate auction, and pulled out the massive collection of Aida fabric I had gathered. My rule was that my stash of fabric couldn't grow bigger than this drawer, so I really had to get stitching so I could buy more.

The photo of the design had it stitched on black, but I had a really deep blue that I thought would work wonderfully. It was 18-count, which was a bit smaller than the pattern called for, but that was fine. Santi had gotten me a great magnifier with a bright lamp for Christmas, and now my middle-aged eyes could handle the smaller stitches.

I gathered the necessary colors from my trays in the trunk at my end of the couch, set up my fabric on my lapstand, and made a cup of chamomile. Then I turned on the TV and decided I would finish *Blacklist*. I was halfway through what I thought was the last season, and the show was fast enough to occupy my brain but not so fast that I had to watch every second.

Bedtime must have required a few stories tonight, or Santi had been a pushover, maybe both because I was almost done with one episode of the show and the shark's dorsal fin when Santi came down the stairs.

"He's out and snoring," he said as she settled next to me on the couch. "Catch me up."

I smiled. Santi claimed to find Reddington, the show's supposed villain, reprehensible, but he never missed an episode if he could help it.

I gave him the rundown on the plastic surgeon and Reddington's surgery and told him about Elizabeth's latest escapades, and then we began another episode together. This time, the criminal was a very old man whose health was quite frail but who successfully conned people, particularly other elderly people, out of their fortunes. He made them believe he could assist them in setting up trusts for the people they loved so that their money would be available to them until they died but would then be preserved for children or grandchildren. But in reality, he simply took the money and moved on.

"That's a good con," Santi said about two-thirds of the way through the show. "People assume the elderly are always innocent because we universally underestimate them. The first case I ever worked on was of a ninety-two-year-old lady who was an expert shoplifter. She could steal anything right out from under anyone and walk out with alarms blaring and all. No one ever suspected her."

"What was the best thing she stole?" I asked.

"A fur coat with matching mittens and hat. She just wore it right out past the guards."

I nodded. "Oh, that's amazing," I said as I stitched. I listened to the show as I worked, but just at the rear of my mind, I could feel the wiggle of something I needed to think about. It would come to light when it was ready, so I let it writhe away back there until then.

Chapter Ten

In the world of raising small children, the adage "The days are long, but the years are short" proved to be completely accurate. Some afternoons felt like decades, but then I'd wake up and realize that the weekend was here again, and Sawyer was off to his dad's after school. Already, it seemed impossible he had been alive for this many years.

Still, after I promised to take good care of Jade, loaded his backpack with the things he wanted to show his dad, and extracted his solemn word that the Wolverine claws would stay in his backpack until he got off the bus at his dad's house, I squeezed back tears and simultaneously breathed a sigh of relief. It seemed that parenting was simply a series of contradictory emotions that I could either come to accept or find a way to feel guilty about forever. I opted for acceptance, wiped my eyes, and went back inside.

Santi was on the phone in the kitchen with a scowl on his face. "Yes, so like a paddle or something?"

I quietly cleaned up from breakfast as I listened to his half of the conversation.

"So, at least two blows?" He nodded as he spoke. "So definitely intentional. Okay, I'll be in soon."

He put down his phone and turned to me. "Olivia McNamara was struck on the back of the head twice with a flat object."

"Like a paddle," I repeated quietly.

"Exactly," he said. "Maybe she was kayaking and got into an argument?" Santi said without any real conviction.

"I suppose that's possible," I said. "There is a put-in spot there. Could it have been that they were fighting as they got in or out of the water?" That kind of scenario was the only thing that made sense because the angles and the logistics of striking someone with a paddle while *on* the river seemed impossible. It was too hard to stand in a kayak, and besides, someone could get away from you more easily than you could sneak up on someone and strike them—at least, that was what I thought from my limited kayaking experience.

Santi nodded to acknowledge I'd spoken, but I could tell he wasn't really hearing me. "You don't think that's what happened, do you?" I said as I put my head on his shoulder and snaked my arm around his waist.

He leaned his head over on mine. "No, I don't. Why would she go with someone to an isolated spot on the river like that if she thought she was in danger? It takes gear and planning to have a river trip, and something about this feels sudden, like a surprise."

I nodded. My husband had a sense of how crimes happened—his mother liked to make it out as some sort of supernatural ability, and I never contradicted her. But my guess was that it was simply Santi's years of work as a police officer that led him to understand things before he really understood why.

"What makes you say that?" I asked, as I did on

almost every case he had that he was able to share with me. It had become a part of our regular conversations, this pantomime of me asking what he could ask himself but didn't and then listening as he told himself what he already knew but hadn't yet articulated.

"Well, first off," he said before taking a long swig from his coffee cup, "she wasn't wearing clothes for being on the water."

"What was she wearing?"

"Jeans, a wool sweater, and boots."

"It has been chilly," I said, taking up my additional part of devil's advocate.

"True, but would you go kayaking or canoeing in all that heavy clothing?"

I shook my head. "No. A rain slicker, maybe. Hat definitely. But not wool or boots."

"Exactly, and if you had worn that and then been hit over the head hard enough to kill you, you probably would have been soaked through," he said, sliding his wallet into his back pocket and picking up his keys.

"She wasn't wet?"

"Dry as a bone on her back. Just her front was wet."

"She drowned in the shallow water because she was unconscious." The thought gave me shivers.

"And she wasn't moved there. The evidence suggests she was killed where we found her."

"So, not in the water and not at another location." I was following his train of thought closely. "Maybe she was just sitting by the water. That's a beautiful spot."

He nodded. "It is," he said very quietly. I could almost see the synapses firing behind his eyes.

I finished wiping the counters as he stood staring into

space, the final stage of his thinking process in these kinds of moments.

The stretch of river where Olivia's body had been found was very beautiful—a wide, flat span of river with a rocky beach that led right to the edge. Sycamores grew on either side of a football field-length opening along the water, and I always felt framed and sheltered by the trees when I sat there. It was a favorite swimming hole for the local kids and teenagers during the summer, but at this time of year, with the trees just barely shooting out the tips of their lime-green leaves, it would have been particularly picturesque. I could almost see Olivia sitting there in her warm sweater and boots, her back against a large rock. Just the idea of it made me calm and then almost immediately sad.

"She was ambushed," I said as my husband leaned toward me to kiss my cheek.

He sighed. "That's what I'm thinking, yeah."

"Someone snuck up on her while she was resting by the river. How awful." The serene image I'd had in mind a few moments earlier went quickly horrific, and I forced myself to think only about the dishes in front of me.

"The question is, did they know she was going to be there and plan on attacking her, or did they just happen to see her and make a spur-of-the-moment decision?" He was headed toward the door, talking as he walked. He turned and waved to me as he stepped through the door. "See you later."

I blew him a kiss, then watched as he got into his cruiser and went up the driveway before I returned to the sink and finished the dishes as I considered what kind of motive or intensity of emotion it would take to go to the trouble of attacking that woman in that remote spot. Even if they just happened to see her, it would have taken some real work to sneak up to her without being seen. The road ran right up to the beach, so she would have seen them coming.

"What if she knew them?" I said aloud, suddenly realizing I had been thinking this was an attack by a stranger. I grabbed my phone and called Santi.

"You okay?" he said when he answered. "Need me to come back?"

"Oh no, but it just occurred to me that Olivia might not have been concerned when her attacker arrived. I mean, if she knew them, maybe she just thought they'd come to say hi."

"I had just gotten to that idea myself. That seems more likely, doesn't it? It would be quite hard to sneak up on someone through all that gravel."

"Exactly, and the fields around the beach there are pretty flat. You can see clear up the river from the road." I had looked at the vista just the day before when I'd driven by.

"Okay, yeah. Thanks, Pais. Talk later."

I put my phone into my back pocket and looked for my boots. I had a beach to visit.

The last time I'd been out to this particular spot was with Sawyer and his dad a few years before. The hard weeks before our separation were difficult for me to revisit since things had been so strained, and I had been so sad. But this memory was a good one. Sawyer had trotted right into the water next to his dad, his diaper immediately sagging almost to his knees. The boys had skipped stones or tried to, and I had marveled at the trees around us.

It was just a bit earlier in the year, so when I slipped off my boots and stepped in, the water was frigid. I quickly pulled my socks back on before jamming my feet into my boots and leaving them unlaced as I slid slowly down a large boulder.

I'd looked carefully for crime scene tape or signs before I even drove up to the beach, but I didn't see anything. Santi had told me that outdoor crime scenes were hard to protect, given that they were subject to the elements. Plus, this was a pretty open spot. It would be hard to cordone it off effectively, especially with the river right there. Someone could just walk up the shallow waterway and onto the beach.

The rock I was sitting against was the one I had imagined Olivia using for her seat, and I had checked it carefully for blood or other markers from the crime and found nothing. I had to admit that it was a little eerie putting myself in the place I'd imagined her to be, but the stone was warm against my back, and the breeze over the water was making the tiny new leaves shiver. It was almost a perfect moment.

With my eyes closed, I let my mind go back to the day Olivia was found here. If I remember correctly, it had been clear like this but a bit chillier, which would explain the woman's sweater. I was in a hoodie and quite comfortable. A wool sweater would have been too much today, but it had probably been perfect that day, especially if the wind was up a bit.

The water danced along its stone, basically making that musical gurgling that had been so often captured poorly on sound machines. I leaned my head back and let myself relax as I imagined Olivia doing the same, back home from the stresses of a high-profile, high-intensity job in LA, only to learn her beloved aunt had been murdered. This moment of respite must have been a very welcome one.

And then, someone had disturbed it. I could imagine

the sound of car tires on the road behind me and the crunch as they pulled partially onto the gravel beach. If she were like me, she probably would have stayed put, assuming the person was just coming to enjoy the water, to throw in a line or two, maybe.

But then they would have said her name. I pictured her sitting forward, looking around the boulder toward where the voice had come from—a smile on her face as she recognized the speaker—and stood to go over and shake hands, say hi, or give them a hug.

The idea of her hugging her killer sent chills down my spine, but I couldn't let the image go. She would reach over to hug the person, and then they struck her on the back of the head.

With what, though? Something they had hidden behind their back? It seemed hard to imagine that they could swing something hard enough to hit her with that much force from that position.

Besides, Olivia had been closer to the water. I stood and walked that way, imagining Olivia and someone else standing there, gazing at the water. They talked quietly, and then, *wham*, the other person smacked her on the back of the head, and Olivia fell face-first into the water.

Something about that didn't seem right either. How would this person keep a weapon sizable enough to knock someone unconscious hidden? I was missing something.

I strode up and down the small beach as I forced myself to concentrate on the sound of the water and the sunlight sparkling off the ripples. I knew myself well enough to know that I wasn't going to force my brain to connect the glimmers I had. I had to let the synapses do their own work.

So I played a game my dad and I had played a lot when I was younger and imagined myself having the best day I could at the stream. It was cool, the early days of autumn, warm enough in the sun but chilly enough to require a sweater. The leaves were still mostly green, but the sycamores had already begun to go yellow and shed their foliage. A breeze was blowing just hard enough to lift my hair around my ears.

I imagined taking off my socks and sneakers and putting my toes into the water, letting them numb with the cold. I saw myself skipping a rock and getting a record six skips. I was just bending down to pick up another rock when, in my mind, I saw a shadow behind me.

I turned around, and there was the man who bagged my groceries, a large branch in his hand, and he was smiling. This man was always sweet to me, so I smiled at him in my imagination. He raised the branch like he was going to throw it in the river, but he swung toward me instead.

With a jolt, I returned to the here and now to find myself standing with my shoes in the stream and my heart racing. My whole body shuddered, and then I felt the pieces click into place. The man at the grocery store, Edwin was his name, was harmless. He was kind and gentle, and since he was developmentally disabled, most people ignored him. But I made a point to speak to him, not because I was something special but because I knew how it felt to be unseen.

The killer had felt that way—underappreciated, disregarded. And Olivia had trusted them. She knew her killer. That was why they got so close.

In a flash, I realized that I had been accurate with my mental vision of the branch and cast my eyes about to see if I could find a likely candidate. The ground was strewn with pale branches that the sycamore had dropped during storms. Many of them were big enough to deal an intense blow, and I knew with certainty that this was the murder weapon.

Santi and his team would have checked the branches nearby, though, so the killer must have carried it away with them, or maybe they chucked it into the stream so it would float away.

But the water was shallow, just a couple of inches of water above the rock bed. A branch of any size wouldn't have floated at all. It would still be sitting there.

That was when I saw it—a branch shaped like a field hockey stick, sitting in the water about ten feet downstream. Close enough to have been flung if someone had a good arm but still far enough away not to seem a likely weapon.

Given that my shoes were already soaked, I waded into the water to the branch and studied it. I expected that any evidence had washed away over the past few days, but I wanted to be sure. And when I leaned over, there was a brownish, reddish slash of color right on the crook of the branch. "Blood," I said aloud and then quickly glanced around to be sure I was alone.

I didn't see anyone, so I quickly snapped a couple of pictures of the branch and waded back out of the water. I didn't bother to dry off before I climbed into the car, slammed it into gear, and took off with dust spinning out behind me. I needed to tell Santi, and I didn't have any signal here.

As soon as I reached the main road, though, my phone showed two bars, and I used voice commands to dial him. Fortunately, my husband was quite used to the speed at which I talked when I was excited, so rather than try to get me to slow down, he simply listened and then said, "You think you found the branch that killed Olivia? Is that right?"

"Yes, I took pictures. I'm texting them now."

"Paisley, pull over at the gas station. I'll meet you there in five minutes." He hung up.

I had been flying down the road, so I was, indeed, just a few hundred feet from the old-fashioned gas station on the way into town. I whipped the car into the gravel parking lot and sat, breathing hard as I watched the old-timer nearby filling his beat-up truck with gas.

"You okay there, Paisley girl," he said as I laid my head against the steering wheel.

"Oh yeah, just fine, Mr. Jenkins. You know me. I get a little carried away sometimes." I let out a coarse laugh that either convinced this old friend of my dad's that I was fine or beyond help because he raised a hand and drove off, passing Santi as the police cruiser pulled in.

Santi walked over and got into the passenger seat of my car. "Show me the pictures," he said.

Some women might have wanted comfort then, but I didn't. I wanted what I'd said to be taken seriously, and Santi did just that. As soon as I showed him the pics, he was back in his cruiser, calling for his deputies to get out to the river and secure the branch.

"Paisley, did anyone see you out there?" Santi was now leaning in my car window, looking very serious.

I shook my head. "I don't think so. No one else was there." I sighed. "But the road does go right by."

He nodded. "Please go home and only leave the house to get Sawyer off the bus. I'm calling Mika to meet you, okay?"

Without a word, I started the car and drove home, still speeding, but at least this time, I recognized it.

Mika pulled in maybe two minutes after me, and we waited at the kitchen table for Sawyer's bus. The two of us popped up and jogged out to meet the boy when we heard the bus coming over the bridge, and we challenged Sawyer to a race back to the house. When he handily beat us, he turned, grinned, and said, "Mom, you ran," which was a testament to the frequency of this activity.

We had a good, if somewhat forced, laugh about my fitness level and then proceeded to make kettle corn—à la powdered mix, not actual kettle—and watch a movie. While Saw and I used the air popper, Mika did a second check of all the doors and also closed the blinds, telling Sawyer it was for our movie night.

Then, the three of us grabbed the extra comforter from my bed and curled up to watch *Woody Woodpecker*, a movie Saw loved because of how much of a prankster the wood-pecker is. Mika and I kept our phones nearby, and Santi gave me updates as he had them—updates I then texted four feet to my right to Mika so that we wouldn't have to answer questions from Sawyer.

My texts were getting more and more filled with excla-mation points as it became clear that the branch I had photographed was nowhere to be found in the stream. Santi had asked me twice to clarify where it had been, and he'd even tried to use my photos to match the rocks around it in the stream. But there was no branch of that shape anywhere to be found.

"I'm sorry, Paisley. I think someone must have gotten here before we did," his final text said. "Be home in fifteen."

As soon as the forwarded message hit Mika's phone, she shivered and wrote back, "Someone saw you!"

I nodded over Sawyer's head. "Not again," I typed into the phone. Sawyer and I had been in a bit of trouble months ago when I'd gotten too close to a murderer during one of my sleuthing expeditions. I was not eager to have that happen again.

As I hit send, I heard tires on the gravel, and Sawyer tried to jump up and run to the front door, expecting it to be Santi. When I slammed him back to the couch with sheer motherly force, I saw tears well up in his eyes, and I looked down at him and apologized. "Just let me check first."

"I've got it," Mika said and headed for the door just as I heard keys in the lock.

"I'm home," Santi said in his best Ward Cleaver voice. "Where are my two favorite people in the world?" This was his usual greeting, and I loved it.

"Oh, I didn't know you cared so much, Santi," Mika said with a laugh just as Sawyer barrelled past her and leapt into Santi's arms.

"We're watching Woody Woodpecker. Come watch with us." It wasn't a question.

"Of course," Santi said. "Just let me put my things away, and I'll be right there."

Mika scooped Sawyer out of Santi's arms and tickled him while she carried him back to the couch. "I am going to tickle you until you pee," she said, and, not for the first time, I was immensely grateful that my best friend was so good with my son.

I watched as Santi hung up all his things in the usual places, but instead of going upstairs to the gun safe, as we had agreed he would when he moved in, he slid his sidearm behind the potholders in the kitchen drawer. "We'll just need to keep Saw out of here until bedtime," he said as he held my eyes. "I need this close tonight."

I shivered. "Of course," I said. "Let's go watch the movie."

I barely noticed the film or even Sawyer's repeated laughter at the bird's antics because my mind was racing with questions for my husband. But I knew it was better to wait, as hard as that was, until Sawyer was asleep. Then, the three of us could talk things through.

As soon as the movie finished, I threw Sawyer over my shoulder and hauled him upstairs to get his "wilds out" before bed. I'd developed this term for my rambunctious little boy on a rainy day when we couldn't get outside. Instead, I'd told him to lay on the bed and wiggle and kick and shake and such until he was tired. It worked like a charm for burning off that last bit of energy, and Sawyer loved it.

Tonight, his wilds were pretty mild, and before I even finished reading *Pirate Stew*, he was drifting off with one arm thrown casually over Jade, who had apparently decided that this was the best bed in the house. I turned on his white noise machine and even bumped the volume up a bit just to be sure he didn't hear us talking and then closed the door to the gentle sound of his breath.

For a long moment, I paused at the top of the stairs as I tried to gather in the kind of peace only my safely sleeping child could give me, and then I went down to hear what exactly in this new hell was going on.

Chapter Eleven

When I walked into the kitchen, I saw a pitcher of margaritas and three glasses and immediately knew this was serious. None of us were big drinkers, especially of hard liquor, but sometimes life did call for tequila.

As I sat at the table beside Santi, Mika poured me a glass and put a lime wedge on the rim. "No salt, I'm afraid, but I'll rectify that situation for next time."

I rolled my eyes. Mika was always stocking my kitchen with the things she thought we were missing, and I had to admit I didn't hate that. It saved me on groceries and trips to the store. Tonight, I was especially glad she'd been steadily building up my liquor cabinet—not really a cabinet, but a dark corner of my pantry—because the warmth of the tequila felt good.

"So, Pais, I was right," Mika said as she sat back down. "Someone did see you."

Santi let out a long, hard breath. "Yes, apparently so." He looked over at me and frowned. "I'm not going to tell you that I don't love that you went there alone, but," he smiled, "I am glad you got photos of the murder weapon. It's not enough for court, but it does clarify some things."

"Like what," I said as I took another small sip of my margarita.

"Well, we had assumed the killer was about Olivia's height because of the direction of the wound, but the branch you photographed makes it more likely the person was smaller."

"You mean they had more arm length because the branch was so big?" I asked.

"That and the angle of it meant they could swing down with it and still hit the top of the head." Santi started to push back his chair, presumably to demonstrate, but one look at my face must have changed his mind. "You know what I mean?"

"I do," I said after swallowing hard. "Okay, that makes sense since Olivia drowned, right? That means they didn't have to hit her that hard."

"Exactly," Santi said. "The blow wasn't what killed her. So the person only had to be strong enough to knock her out."

I sat back and thought for a minute. "Okay, but whoever killed Ms. McNamara actually killed her with the blow, right?"

Santi studied me. "That's right. What are you thinking?"

I shook my head. "I'm not sure. But these two deaths have to be connected. It's just not feasible that aunt and niece would die just days apart by coincidence."

Mika nodded. "I'd say that's true." She glanced over at Santi, who was scowling. "I know. I know. It's not evidence. But let's just go with it for the moment."

He didn't look happy, but my husband nodded. "Okay.

If we're supposing, let's suppose it is the same killer. What does that mean?"

I wasn't sure if his question was rhetorical or not, but I decided to answer. "It means that either the person didn't get the force they wanted when they hit Olivia, or they hit Ms. McNamara too hard."

Santi nodded but then immediately began shaking his head. "That is one possibility," he said. "But there's another, too. Presumably, they didn't use the same murder weapon, right?"

A small smile turned up one corner of Mika's mouth. "Right. They surely didn't carry a sycamore branch around with them."

I closed my eyes and tried to imagine the scene at the river again, to feel what I was feeling when I was there. "No, that's right. They picked up the branch at the river because it turned out they needed it. They hadn't planned to need it, though."

My eyes flew open. "They didn't go there to kill Olivia."

"Okay, tell me how you got there, Pais," Santi said as he put his hand over mine.

"They were just going to talk to Olivia, maybe, but then she wouldn't go along with what they said." I shook my head. "I'm totally guessing now."

"Nope, don't do that," Mika said. "Don't undercut your own thoughts. What's making you say that?"

I smiled at my friend. "Okay, when I was at the river today, it was so peaceful, a great place to focus and relax, to think. So, what if our killer saw Olivia sitting there, like they saw me today, and decided to see if they could talk to her, convince her of something."

Santi stood and began pacing. "But she wasn't convinced. She wouldn't agree to whatever they wanted."

"And they killed her then," Mika said with a drop of her shoulders. "So she definitely knew them."

"Well, not definitely," I said. "It's just a guess, but it seems to fit, right?"

"It does, and it's a good working theory. I'll talk with Forest tomorrow to see what we can find in terms of evidence of that." Santi sighed. "But now, I really need to go to bed."

I emptied the remaining half of my margarita into the sink. "Me, too." I turned and grabbed a cover to go over the top of the margarita pitcher. "I'll finish these this weekend. I'll have salt by then."

Mika laughed. "Yes. Yes, you will."

———

To say that my sleep was restless that night would be an understatement. I kept dreaming about women being hit over the head by branches, tea kettles, and even a brick. When I woke up, I felt like I'd been in one of those naps that never really became sleep. It was going to be a long day.

Fortunately, Sawyer was in a good mood and began his questions about Bigfoot early. He had the best theories about what the cryptid could actually be, and by the time he got on the bus, Santi and I had considered everything from foot size to fur type as he pondered everything from the possibility of wolves that walked on two legs to North American gorillas. If anyone was going to solve this mystery, it was my boy, and I was happy to help. Bigfoot was easier than murder, for sure.

I had a bunch of online listings to catch up on, and I was pretty behind on answering emails. So I checked in at the shop and decided to work from home, maybe from the front porch if the sun warmed things up enough. First, though, the floor needed to be vacuumed, or I would lose my mind. I just couldn't stand the feel of grit on my bare feet.

I sent Sawyer outside to play with Jade and got the vacuuming done while resisting the urge to do the deepest cleaning ever done to a human's habitation, then sat down at my desk. Emails were usually pretty quick and easy to handle since most ran through the shop and were handled by Claire. The only messages she ever left for me were those people who wrote to me specifically, maybe about a newsletter article or wanting to know the story of a particular piece.

The first message waiting for me was about a beautiful stained glass window I'd obtained from a robber baron's mansion a couple of months back. The writer wanted to know if I had any more information about the family because he thought they might be relatives. I told him what I knew and made a note to do a little more digging for a future newsletter.

However, the second note wasn't so easy, and I immediately forwarded it to Santi and waited for his call. The email read:

Ms. Sutton,
I see you have, once again, found yourself embroiled in the darker side of life in Octonia. I don't know how you can handle all this murder and intrigue, but you seem to be fairing well if looks are to be believed. In this McNamara debacle, however, you are stirring waters that are best left still. I see through your shallow ploy to discuss the house as a way of quietly gathering data about its owners, but that tactic will not work with me nor, I fervently hope, with anyone else who knew Viola

back in those early days. That house was her deepest love, at least later in her life, and she kept its secrets close, as they should stay.

Please, out of respect for the long-standing members of this community, cease this useless search and let sleeping dogs lie.

Sincerely,

A Comfortably Sleeping Dog

The message was a threat, certainly, but an intriguing one. Clearly, this person knew something and obviously didn't want me to know what they knew. But why write the note at all, then? Why stir the waters further if you'd rather them be left undisturbed?

My phone rang, and I picked up to hear Santi say, "You okay?"

"Yeah. It's a weird message, isn't it?"

"Absolutely. Part threat and part request for you to look further? Is that what you're thinking?"

"Exactly," I said. "I think this is a note from someone who really wants us to look harder, but who can't say that?"

"Yes, that's what I'm thinking. So you know what this means?"

"I quit investigating and make snickerdoodles?" I said with a laugh.

He chuckled. "I never turn down a cookie, but we have to keep digging. You, however, have to do it carefully, Paisley. We're coming by the house every half-hour or so just to be sure all is quiet, and the school has been notified to be extra vigilant about Saw. But if someone doesn't like what you're doing. . ."

I sighed. "I know. But they can't see what I do from home, right?" The pause at the end of the line made me nervous. "Right?"

"As far as I know. We don't exactly have the greatest

equipment here at the office, but I don't think our house has been bugged or anything. And you keep your computer secure, right?"

"Passwords on everything since my business stuff is on here. I think it's safe."

"Okay, good. So, keep digging from home. I'll come by around lunch to check in." He laughed. "Maybe they'll be some of those snickerdoodles?"

"Don't push your luck, mister," I said, even as I grabbed the cinnamon and cream of tartar from the baking cabinet. "See you in a couple of hours."

I poured my final cup of coffee and grieved, as my morning routine dictated, the empty French press, and then I went and stood by the front windows. Suddenly, working on the porch seemed a little more risky, but when I saw a patrol car slow as it passed the end of my driveway, I decided I was as safe on my porch as I was in my house and gathered my sweater, coffee mug, and laptop and headed out, Beauregard close behind me.

While he stalked the sedum plants in front of the porch in case an early cricket or grasshopper was nearby, I set up my workstation on the glass table by my rocking chair and went to work. The emailer had made a point about Viola's house holding secrets, and while I thought that we had exhausted the physical house's secrets, given that we'd ripped open the walls and such, I wanted to be sure.

"Xzanthia," I said after she answered. "Do you have a minute to help me with something?"

The call only lasted a couple of moments, but within ten minutes, I had scans of the blueprints of the cottage design for the McNamara place and the other four similar houses along that street. Xzanthia had found them in a collection of architectural records when she remembered that the houses were all built by the same man at about the same time.

"Look carefully at the front, west parlor, Paisley," Xzanthia's note in the email said.

So, of course, I started there, and it took me quite a few minutes to see it. But there, just behind the wainscotting walls of the room to the left of the front door, was a small alcove. It took me a while to see it because it looked just like a shadow on the blueprint, not an actual space. But when I zoomed in, it was clear—there was a small, secret room behind that panel.

I called Xzanthia back immediately. "How did I miss that when I was there?"

She chuckled. "My guess is that there's a locking mechanism that even your pounding didn't release it. Should we go take a look?"

I glanced down at my phone. Ten. I still had a couple of hours before Santi got home. He wouldn't be thrilled that I went out, but I would remind him I was with Xzanthia and that I'd be back by lunch, just sans snickerdoodles.

As I'd predicted, he wasn't happy but agreed to shift the check-in patrols to the McNamara place for the remainder of the morning and even hinted at coming over himself. I called Mrs. Cubbins as I drove into town and asked if I could get one last look inside the house, just in case I'd missed anything. I didn't want to tell her what we'd found until I'd had a chance to look inside. I still couldn't shake the sense that she and her husband weren't being forthcoming about everything.

I apparently played off the request with enough nonchalance because she readily agreed and reminded me of the code for the lockbox on the door. "Just know that my interior designer will be there about noon for an initial walk-through. If you could, please be gone by then. She's not entirely thrilled that we let you take so much from the house and, well," she said after clearing her throat, "I don't want her to give you any trouble."

"Understood," I said, although I couldn't blame the designer for being upset. As far as I was concerned, I had taken the best parts of the house when we'd salvaged there. "I'll be out long before then."

Xzanthia was walking up just as I parked, and together, we opened the front door and immediately went to the corner by the columns just off the central hallway, the place where the blueprints indicated was a secret space. I looked carefully at the lathe and plaster behind the wainscotting, but I couldn't see any cracks or places for hinges.

"Do you see anything?" I asked my friend.

She stepped forward and carefully studied the wall before taking out her phone and looking at the blueprints again. "No. Not exactly. Maybe it was boarded up or just an idea, something that didn't get built in here."

I had put a small crowbar into my purse before I left the house, just in case we had to pry open a hidden door. I took it out and looked at it. "Should we open up the wall?"

Xzanthia studied the space again. "No, let's not. If there's nothing there, we will just be making more work for everyone." She walked back to the front door. "I have another idea."

Puzzled and not a little frustrated, I followed her out the front door and down the front walk, where she made a right-hand turn away from the historical society. She walked briskly, and I jogged to catch up just as she made another right-hand turn into the next walkway up the street. I glanced at the house ahead of us and smiled. It was nearly identical to the McNamara place. "You're going to see if they have a secret room?"

She winked at me. "Now, just go along, dear." She rang the doorbell, and a woman in her forties opened it.

"Can I help you?" she said.

"My name's Xzanthia Lewis, and I am the director of the local historical society. This is Paisley Sutton. You may know her from her articles in the paper or her local architectural salvage business."

The woman didn't look to be much inclined toward history or architecture, given the eyebrow she raised at us, but she didn't send us away.

"We have actually come across some information that we thought might interest you and wondered if we might have a minute of your time," Xzanthia said in her sweetest Southern voice.

The woman sighed and stepped out of the doorway. "Sure," she said. "I have a *few* minutes." The emphasis on the *few* wasn't lost on me.

We stepped into a front entrance that was a replica of what the Cubbins house had been before I took it apart—wainscotting, beautiful built-ins, and even the same mantel pieces. It was spectacular, and I couldn't help saying so.

At my praise, the woman softened a bit. "We do love it. The first few years we lived here, the kids were small, and we spent most of our time keeping them from writing, chewing, or banging on the woodwork. But we managed, and now, we get to enjoy it."

I ran my fingers over the mantel in the room we were interested in, looking at it more closely. "You know I salvaged from the house next door?"

She gasped. "What? Is it being torn down?"

"Oh no, no. They're keeping the exterior as is, but the

new owners wanted a more contemporary interior. So I am now the owner of most of the woodwork." I smiled. "If you ever need to replace anything, I'm happy to give you what you need. I'd love to have a small part in preserving your place."

My offer melted the final coolness in her tone, and she smiled. "I may just take you up on that. But now, what can I do for you?" She pointed to a settee by the front windows.

Xzanthia took out her phone and showed her the blueprints. "We think you might have a secret closet or room just there?" she said, pointing one long, fuschia nail to the corner across from us.

"A secret room?" The woman practically giggled. "What a treat! Where do we start?"

"Well, if there's a room in there, the builder must have included a way to open it," I said as we moved toward the corner. "Is everything here yours?" I looked at the plants and knick-knacks that adorned the small table and the shelf by the column in that area.

The woman looked at her décor and nodded. "Yep, everything is ours." She slowly spoke as she scanned the vase, the potted plant, and the golden monkey bookends that framed three leather-bound books.

"Okay, then it must be built into the house," Xzanthia said. "Let's see if anything looks different before we start pulling on things."

I nodded. "Yes. Maybe the woodwork will reveal more than the lathe next door did."

"Ah, so you're thinking if we have one, then they do too," our host said. "Smart." She didn't seem put off at all, so with a shared glance, the three of us began to study the wainscot carefully.

After a few minutes of futility, I said, "I don't see any

cracks in the wood that stand out, nothing shaped like a door at least."

Both Xzanthia and the woman shook their heads.

"All right, let's test things with our fingers," I suggested. "That's how it works in the movies, right?"

Xzanthia rolled her eyes but didn't hesitate to start running her fingers over the woodwork. Soon, all three of us were checking every inch of the beautiful wood to see if we could feel anything to show us how to open the room—presuming there was a room, of course.

But after every inch of the entire wall had been scanned by three sets of hands and three pairs of eyes, even I had to admit that we were probably not going to find anything.

"I'm Caroline, by the way," our host said. "I just realized I hadn't told you my name."

I started laughing. "Wow, we are so rude."

"Not at all," Caroline said. "I purposefully didn't introduce myself at first. I thought you were going to ask me for money."

Xzanthia laughed. "Not on this visit." She winked. "But I understand. I typically hide when someone rings my bell."

Just then, a boy who looked to be about ten came from the back of the house. "Mom, are we having lunch soon?"

"Thad, you are quite capable of making yourself some lunch. Can't you see we have guests?"

Thad looked appropriately abashed and hung his head. "Sorry, Mom." Then he looked up. "What are you doing?"

It wasn't exactly the most polite question, but from a kid, it was totally expected.

When his mom gave me a nod, I turned to Thad and said, "Well, we were looking for a secret room, but it looks like we were wrong in thinking it might be here."

Thad's face turned a shade of red that resembled a very ripe strawberry, and he said, "You didn't find it?"

Xzanthia glanced at me. "No, we didn't. But we'd like to. It might help us help some friends of ours." She fixed Thad with a stare so intense that a fully grown adult would have probably shuddered.

"Oh," Thad shuffled his feet. "Well, okay then."

"Okay then, what?" Thad's mother said. "What do you know?"

Thad walked a couple of steps further into the room, then reached for the pillar nearest the corner where we had been looking. "I found this a couple of years ago when I was goofing around with some friends." He put his hands on the column and turned it a quarter of the way around. As he did, a click sounded in the exact corner of the wall we'd been studying, and a door swung inward.

Behind the wall was a small room, about the size of a typical coat closet, and Thad had clearly made it his own. It was covered with anime posters and had a rickety old rocker and a small camping lantern. On the crate next to the chair, Thad had an impressive collection of anime. He'd made it his haven.

"Thad, why didn't you tell me?" Caroline looked somewhere between hurt and angry.

"It was just my own space, Mom. Nothing fancy and completely safe. Just a place where I could hang out and read." He shrugged his shoulders. "I wasn't hurting anyone."

This was obviously a family discussion, but before we left, I really wanted just a quick second to peek inside the room. "Do you mind if I look inside? We're hoping there might be a similar room next door," I said to Thad. I didn't want him to think I was prying into his stuff. I kind of thought it was awesome that he'd made himself a little reading cave.

"Please," Caroline said. "And maybe now you can open the one next door?"

I nodded. "I hope so."

Inside the room, the walls were plastered just like the rest of the house. Nothing fancy. There was no electricity, but there seemed to be a small ventilation hole that ran—if the layout of this house was the same as the one next door, which the blueprints seemed to indicate—opened to the crawl space under the stairs.

But otherwise, it was just a secret room, a very cool thing but not particularly revealing. "Well, let's go see about our room," I said to Xzanthia after she took her turn examining the space.

"You'll let us know?" Caroline asked as she walked us to the door.

"Of course," I said. "And please thank Thad for us. He really saved the day."

She smiled and looked over her shoulder. "I will after I let him sweat it a bit. We don't do secrets in our family."

I smiled. "Now it's not a secret anymore."

"Exactly," she said and gently closed the door.

Xzanthia and I practically ran next door, but we stopped short when we noticed the fancy sports car in the driveway. "The interior designer must be here," I said quietly. "Do we go in?"

Without hesitation, Xzanthia shook her head. "No. We need to see this without anyone else around except Santi."

"Agreed. And he may just be our way back in the

house." I glanced at my watch. I was due to meet him in about fifteen minutes. "Call you in a couple of hours?"

"You better," Xzanthia said. "I've been dreaming of finding a secret passageway or room in a house since I read *The Mysterious Benedict Society*. I'm not going to miss out."

I laughed and gave her a quick hug before hustling to my car and heading home. I really needed to catch Santi up.

Chapter Twelve

It was only as I was making the last turn off the "big road," as Sawyer called it, onto our "little road" that I noticed the gray sedan following me. It had been behind me since I left town, but since we only had four major roads out here, I hadn't been concerned until it turned onto my road. I knew most of the cars that went with the houses along here, and this wasn't one of them. I was being followed.

The typical wisdom in this situation was that I should go anywhere but home, but given that I knew a police cruiser was going to be sitting in my driveway when I got there, I did the opposite of the conventional wisdom and sped up toward my driveway while also asking my phone to call my husband.

"Santi, gray sedan, older car, following me toward the house now. I can't make out the plate."

"All right, I'll be ready," he said. "ETA?"

"Three and a half minutes," I said without hesitation. Sawyer asked me incessantly how long until we got home every time we turned onto our road, so I now had a fairly good estimate for most of the major landmarks along the way. Just now, we were passing the large Lego chicken in our neighbor's yard, and that meant 210 seconds. If Saw were with me, he'd count to 210.

Thus, exactly three and a half minutes later, I put on my blinker and turned into my driveway, pulling my car past Santi's cruiser as he sat behind the wheel with the window down. "Go inside. Stay there."

I nodded and did as I was told. I normally didn't take orders well, but I listened when they were from my husband, who was protecting my life. I drove to the house, jumped out of the car, and ran inside just as I heard Santi's tires peel out.

When I ran to the window, I could just make out his car as it crossed the railroad bridge, presumably in pursuit of the car that had been tailing me. I waited and listened at the window to see if I could hear anything up the road, but all that reached my ears was the sound of the sawdust blower from the cabinetry shop up the road.

I plopped down in a dining room chair and laid my head on the table as I took some deep breaths to soothe my nervous system. Then, I heard tires on the gravel and jumped up, my defense systems zooming right back to activation.

It was a police car, but not Santi's. Deputy Forest stepped out and came to the door. "I'm here until the sheriff gets back," he said.

Of course, I thought, Santi called him. "All right. Would you like some tea?"

"Well, yes, please," the deputy said. "Mind if I sit here?" He pointed to the table on the porch.

"Please. Mind if I join you? I don't think I can concentrate on anything at the moment."

"Sure thing. Maybe you can fill me in on what happened?" he said.

I knew that Santi had probably given him all the most pertinent information about the car following me already, but I was happy to ramble on about the morning to him just to fill the silence.

As expected, Deputy Forest was particularly excited about the potential secret room in the McNamara house, although I couldn't tell if it was the same kind of excitement I had—"ooh, a secret room"—or more of the "there might be evidence" in there, excitement. Either way, he was eager to see it as soon as possible.

I had hoped that could happen right after lunch, but as Santi's absence stretched on, it seemed more and more likely that we were going to be waiting here for the rest of the afternoon. "Santi's okay, right?" I finally asked after a prolonged silence had brought up all my anxieties.

"Oh yes, he's fine," Deputy Forest said confidently. "He would have radioed for help if he needed me."

"But his radio is in his car, what if—"

The deputy didn't let me finish. "The radio is tied to his phone, which he always keeps on him. He's fine, Paisley."

Whether his confidence in my husband's safety was bravado or knowledge, I didn't care. Something about the solidness of his statement eased my nerves a bit.

Then, a car turned into the driveway, and I looked up to see Santi pulling in. I started to run over to see him, but the deputy put a hand on my arm. "He's got someone in the back. Wait here," he said.

I squinted at the tinted windows of the cruiser, but I couldn't make anything out in the back. Forest was a great deal younger than I was, so maybe his eyesight was better. But I was hoping that maybe there was some secret signal officers used with each other to indicate they had a person in custody.

For a couple of minutes, Santi and Forest talked together by the car, and then Santi turned and opened the back door. Out stepped Lucy Somerall, looking tiny in her cardigan, mid-calf skirt, and sensible walking shoes.

I couldn't believe my eyes, and when Santi walked her over to me, I found I couldn't even form words.

Fortunately, Lucy saved me the trouble. "I'm so sorry, Paisley. I didn't mean to scare you. I simply meant to follow you home so we could talk." She blushed. "I can now see how that might have been a bit intimidating."

I stared at her a moment before my mouth caught up to my ears. "You were tailing me?" I couldn't believe it.

"Yes, and again, I'm so sorry." She looked up at the sheriff. "Are you going to charge me?"

Santi actually laughed. "With what?"

"Stalking? Aggravated something or other?" the tiny woman said.

This time, Forest laughed. "Want me to book her, boss?" he said with a chuckle.

"I don't think that will be necessary, but don't do that again, okay?" Santi gave Ms. Somerall a stern warning.

"Absolutely not," she said. "I should have known better, but this situation has me all flummoxed."

It was only then that I noticed her hands were shaking. "Lucy, come sit. We were just having some iced tea. Would you like some?"

"Is it sweet?" she asked.

"Is there any other kind?" I said with a smile as I took her arm and led her to the porch. "Please sit. I'll be right back with two more glasses."

In a town larger than Octonia, it would have been

trouble to have both the available police officers in one place relaxing, but then, in a town larger than Octonia, there would be more than two police officers. Either way, neither Santi nor Forest seemed inclined to move along, so I grabbed two of the dining room chairs and brought them to the porch before I poured the tea.

When I sat down, Santi had his notebook out, as did Forest, and I took that as a signal we were into official police business now. Still, I was glad Santi had waited. He began, "Now, Ms. Somerall, please tell us why you were following Paisley."

Lucy looked chagrined and a bit peeved—at least, that was what I took the pursing of her lips to mean. "I told you all this when you stopped me, Sheriff. I simply wanted to talk with Paisley, see if I could explain things."

"Explain what?" I said, too eager and agitated to let the police handle this one.

"Explain what happened with Olivia."

I squinted at the old woman across from me. "What do you mean what happened to Olivia?"

"At the river, dear. I've wanted to explain, but Abigail didn't want to say anything." Lucy blushed. "And I hate to anger her."

"What happened?" I said, more tersely than I had intended. "Please."

Lucy sighed. "We just wanted to talk to her, to ask her to please clarify things with you about Viola, explain that her aunt was quite a capable woman, a good woman."

I stared blankly as my mind tried to tie things together.

"But Abigail has such a temper, and I wasn't big enough to stop her." Lucy bit her lip. "I tried to tell her we needed to turn ourselves in, but she insisted that wasn't necessary.

That we were just two old ladies, and no one would miss Olivia."

Santi was taking notes, and I looked down to see him write, "Abigail struck the blow."

I blinked rapidly. "Wait, are you saying that Abigail Toperman killed Olivia?"

Lucy nodded. "Yes, dear. Keep up."

Deputy Forest laid a hand on my arm as he felt me tense. Good thing, too, or I would have laid into the old biddy who had watched Olivia die and not reported the crime. "You were there?" I said as calmly as I could.

Lucy rolled her eyes in frustration, and Forest pressed down more firmly on my forearm. "Yes, that's what I'm saying. I tried to stop her, but Abigail was bigger and stronger. Before I knew it, she had the branch and had killed Olivia."

I took a deep breath and looked at Santi. He was still taking notes but looked up at me a moment later and nodded. "So, what did you do when she hit her?"

"I stepped in between them," Lucy said, her voice quieter now. "But Abigail just shoved me out of the way. Gave me this nasty scratch." She held up her arm like Sawyer did when he hurt himself.

I could feel my anger rising, but I held my tongue as Santi continued to ask questions.

"And Abigail hit her with?"

Lucy sighed. "As I said before, it was a tree branch." She tapped Santi's notebook. "Really, Sheriff, you should have taken notes the first time."

My husband took a long breath in through his nose and then sighed. "And after Abigail hit her, what happened?"

"Well, the girl was dead, and there wasn't anything we

could do. Abigail insisted we leave and that no good would come of us getting caught."

I stared at Santi until he met my gaze and sighed again. "Go ahead," he said quietly.

Normally, I was a very compassionate person, too compassionate sometimes, and I almost never wanted to cause anyone pain. But this woman was sitting here acting as if she could simply explain that her best friend had clubbed a young woman and then go home to take a nap or whatever she did on a weekday afternoon. Her nonchalance was infuriating, and my rare mean streak rose.

"Olivia wasn't dead when you left. She drowned. You could have helped her, but you just left her there to die." I spat the words and immediately regretted it when Lucy's face shifted from shock to tears.

"W-what?" she whispered.

"I'm afraid Olivia wasn't dead, Ms. Somerall," Santi said. "She was unconscious, yes, but she died sometime later of asphyxiation."

Lucy crumpled against the table then, and she began to sob. "I didn't know," she said. "I didn't know."

———

Forest took Ms. Somerall back to the sheriff's office to charge her as an accessory to murder. My rage had subsided and been overtaken by my usual sympathy, so I had asked if that was necessary, but Santi had assured me it was. But he'd also said they wouldn't keep her. She had, of course, been trying to confess, if in a somewhat unusual way.

"Oh good," I said, but there was a nagging feeling of dread at the back of my mind even as I spoke. I walked into the living room and picked up my sewing. Sometimes, stitching shook the cobwebs loose enough for me to understand what my brain was trying to tell me.

Santi knew me well enough by now to understand that if I was cross-stitching in the middle of the day, I was thinking about something. So he set about doing what he always did when I needed time—he cleaned. It had been a beautiful surprise when we'd started seriously dating that the times I most needed to be still and focused were often the same times he needed to keep moving.

So, while I began stitching a clownfish for Sawyer's picture, that man vacuumed, dusted, and even cleaned the bathroom. I tried to help when he began folding the laundry, but he literally smacked my hand away. "Fine then," I said and picked up my cloth.

I was a few hundred stitches in when the annoying concern zoomed to the forefront of my thoughts. "Abigail!" I shouted as I dropped my needle onto the pin holder and pivoted to face Santi, who stopped in the middle of folding a pair of my oldest underwear.

"Lucy can't tell Abigail she confessed," I said, the image of one older woman bludgeoning the other to death playing like a film through my mind.

Santi nodded and kept folding.

"You're not concerned?" I said with a squeak in my voice as I watched him pick up a stack of socks and begin matching them into pairs. "You're not concerned," I said more quietly as I observed his calm.

"I asked Forest to call Lucy's daughter over in Richmond, and she's on her way to pick up her mother from the police station." He looked over at me. "I've done this before, you know?"

I sighed. "Of course, you thought of that. My brain just

finally settled enough for me to realize that Lucy might be in danger. Sorry I shouted."

He winked at me. "One of the reasons I love you—you don't let things go until you figure them out." He finished the sock pile and filled the laundry basket with our clean clothes. "But maybe I can help ease your mental load a bit and tell you that Lucy also explained that she had seen you down at the river and went down to move the branch after you left. To protect Abigail," she said.

"Oh," I said. "That makes her even more culpable, doesn't it?"

Santi grinned at me with a twinkle in his eye. "It might if she hadn't put the branch in her car."

"She saved it?" I couldn't believe what I was hearing. "Why?"

He shrugged. "She kept saying it was to protect Abigail."

"But you don't think so?"

"Could be, I guess"—he shrugged again—"but sometimes, we say what we think we need to say but do what we need to do."

I looked carefully at my husband's handsome face, made even more attractive, in my opinion, by his recent addition of a close-shaved beard. "You think she feels guilty turning Abigail in but knew she needed to?"

"I do," he said as he picked up the laundry basket. "And now, we have a murderer to arrest."

"You're going to arrest Abigail Toperman now?" I stood up, too, aiming to follow him out the door even though I knew that wasn't really protocol.

He stopped, handed me the laundry basket, and said, "*I* am. You are not. Forest is coming to pick me up soon. I'm leaving the cruiser here just for appearances. It won't take long, but I don't want to take any chances."

I shifted the laundry basket to my hip. "Okay, but be careful."

"I never underestimate anyone, Pais, you know that. This woman killed someone. I'll be on alert." He leaned down and kissed me. "Do you mind putting that away?"

I laughed. "Okay, but you know that's breaking my 'leave it in the basket for two weeks' rule?"

Within a half-hour, Forest had picked up Santi, and I had settled back down with tea and TV to stitch for the little bit of time left until Sawyer got home. Now that we knew who was responsible for Olivia's murder, we just had to figure out who had killed Viola. It seemed unlikely that Abigail had killed her best friend, but then I hadn't pegged her for a killer at all.

About five minutes before Sawyer was due home, I packed up my sewing and walked up the driveway. Within moments, I heard the bus's engine coming up the road from the east, and just then, a white pickup pulled into my driveway and parked next to me. I walked over to see who it was, only to find Abigail Toperman smiling at me. "Well, dear, it looks like I'm just in time. Sawyer's bus driver keeps a tight schedule."

At that moment, the bus stopped at the end of my driveway and discharged my son, who ran to me for his usual hug and then said, "Who's that?"

"I'm your mom's friend, Abi," she said. "We were just going to get some ice cream. Why don't you both hop in?"

I started to push Sawyer down the driveway, but Abi

tapped the windshield with something loud. I glanced back to see her brandishing a revolver. "Come on. I think they have my favorite—cookie dough."

With my hand still on Saw's shoulder, I steered him to the car and climbed in ahead of him so that I was between him and this mad woman. He hesitated at the door. "Mom, I don't have a car seat in here."

Leave it to my boy to be safety conscious when his life is in danger. "It's okay, Saw. Just this once," I said as casually as I could.

He studied me carefully and then got into the truck.

"Very good," Abigail said. "I know this great place over by the mountains."

I slipped my arm around Sawyer to comfort myself as much as him and stared straight ahead.

"Maybelle's, you mean?" Saw said. "I love that place. My dad takes me there all the time."

"That is the place, Sawyer. Smart boy. I love their ice cream." Abigail's voice was so cheerful it was eerie.

Sawyer seemed just fine, though, and said, "Are we going to the one in town or the one out by the hollow?"

Abigail turned to look at him for a moment. "Does it matter?"

"Not really," Sawyer said with a shrug. "The one in town doesn't have as many flavors, though."

A small smile played on Abigail's lips. "Good thing we're going out to the mountains then," she said. "We want you to have as many choices as you can."

It was only then that I saw Sawyer holding his watch close to his mouth as he chewed on the band. It was the kind of thing a kid would do, totally typical, except my kid didn't chew on his watch. He knew better. It was a very expensive watch that was actually a phone, a phone programmed with just four numbers: mine, his dad's, his grandparents', and Santi's.

I squeezed his shoulder. "Off to the mountains we go then," I said, hoping Santi was still on the line. I didn't think we had a chance in hell of going to get ice cream, but at least we maybe had a direction.

Sure enough, we headed west to the main north-south road and headed south before pulling into Maybelle's for ice cream. When Abigail parked the car, she said, "I'm taking Sawyer in for ice cream. Wait here."

It felt like someone pushed iced water into my veins, and I appreciated the drama of my child when he latched onto my arm and said, "I'm not going without my mom. She needs ice cream, too."

I looked down into his face and could see he was scared. His eyes were wide and bright, but he kept it together. "Come on, Mom," he said with a level of playfulness I didn't think he was capable of and tugged me out of the truck.

Behind me, I heard Abigail huff, but she didn't know the level of stubbornness my child could display. She wasn't going to win this battle. "Go pick out your ice cream, Sawyer. I need to talk to your mom for a minute," she said as soon as we were inside.

My child, loyal to his core, was also five, and the ice cream counter was just too tempting. When he looked up at me, and I gave a small nod, he ran over and stood on his tippy-toes to look at the flavors. And that was the last I saw of him before Abigail pushed the gun into my back and said, "He'll be fine here. They'll call the sheriff. Now, we need to go."

I planted my feet. "No, I'm not leaving him here."

"You are," she said, "if you don't want him to see his mother die."

Few things would motivate me to walk away from my child when he was alone, but that was one of them. I couldn't leave Sawyer with that last image of me, so I let Abigail lead me back through the door and into the truck. *Santi, please come quickly*, I prayed.

And just as Abigail turned the truck onto a side road that headed back east, I caught a glimpse of a police light coming at breakneck speed and let out a long sigh. Sawyer was safe. Now, I only had to think about getting home to him.

Fortunately, Abigail was too concentrated on hauling tail to wherever we were going to notice the police cars, and I didn't keep my gaze fixed in that direction too long. Instead, I decided to do the only thing I knew to do—get her talking.

I had no way of calling for help, so I was going to have to rely on Sawyer and Santi to find me, which meant I had to stay alive long enough for them to do that. "Abigail," I paused, "do you mind if I call you that?"

Her face softened for a brief moment, maybe because I had used good manners, a trait that most older Southern folk really appreciate, and she said, "Sure. Why not?"

"All right, so what are you doing? Why are you doing this?" It was a bold question, but I hoped she'd answer.

She smiled, and I saw real menace in her face for the first time. "You'll need to be more specific by what you mean by *this*, dear. That nonspecific pronoun could really apply to a lot of things."

"Okay, let's start with this one. Why did you kill Olivia?"

She didn't even hesitate. "Because she had something that was mine, and she wouldn't tell me where it was."

"What did she have?" I asked, maybe too fast, because Abigail took her eyes off the road and glared at me.

"None of your business," she said. "But I waited a long time to get what was mine, and those McNamaras wouldn't give it up."

I took a deep breath. "You tried to get it from Viola first," I said. "But she didn't want to give it to you either."

"Now you're catching on. She was a dear friend, but a woman has to have principles. I felt bad about it, but I did what had to be done."

"How did you kill her?" I figured I might as well satisfy my curiosity if I was going to die anyway, and if I somehow made it out of this, I wanted to be able to have all the facts straight for Santi. "You hit Olivia with a stick, I know. But that didn't kill her. So you must have used something heavier for Viola."

Abigail flinched. "What do you mean it didn't kill her? That girl is dead. I saw the coroner's van leave the river."

I don't really know what possessed me to say it, but I told what was maybe the ballsiest lie of my life. "Oh, the coroner did come, but they were able to revive her. She almost drowned, though." I tried to sound casual, like I was just relaying facts, even though I could see Abigail fidgeting in the seat next to me.

"Well, if she's not dead, where is she? She hasn't been home. If she had, someone would have found what I did to the place?"

"You ransacked her house looking for whatever this thing is?" I asked.

"And it's nowhere. Just means I have to keep looking." Abigail's jaw was tight.

"But maybe Olivia could tell you, I mean, you already tried to kill her. That had to have scared her, right?"

166

This time, Abigail turned most of her body in the seat and looked at me before whipping the car back to the center of the road a moment later. "You may have a point," she said.

"I know where she is," I said, making *that* the most brazen untruth of my life. "If you let me go, I can tell you where she is."

Abigail scoffed. "You're not going anywhere. You already know more than you should have because of Lucy. She has always been weak, and now, her weakness means I have to clean up this mess."

I immediately thought of Sawyer, of how he could identify Abigail, but I didn't say anything. If she wanted to underestimate my kid, I'd let her. "Well, I guess there's no reason for me to tell you where she is then," I said, not sure exactly what kind of game I was playing here but determined to keep it going if it meant I stayed alive.

"This right here, that's enough reason." Abigail pointed the gun at my knee and pulled back the hammer.

I screamed and moved my leg against the door frame, practically climbing onto the seat.

Abigail started to laugh. "I see you're motivated. Now, where is she?"

My heart was pounding through my throat, and I could barely think, let alone lie well. So, I said the first thing that came to mind. "Olivia's staying at her aunt Viola's old place."

"Liar!" Abigail said with such venom that I could almost feel the word hit my face. "Dolores would have told me if she was there. Now, where is she really?"

My mind tried to put together how Dolores Cubbins tied into all this, but I couldn't figure that out and still keep this charade going. So I just blurted out the next thing I could think of, "Santi's old house."

My husband's house had been sold months ago, but the owners were in DC most of the time, so Santi and I still had a key since we had agreed to be their gardeners and caretakers when they weren't home. "She's staying there until the case is solved."

"Smart girl," Abigail said as she gunned the engine, and I wasn't sure if she was talking about me or Olivia. "His place is over in town, right?"

I nodded. It wasn't surprising Abigail knew where he'd lived. Most everyone knew where almost everyone lived in Octonia. But still, it unsettled me a little. I didn't like this woman knowing where the people I loved lived, and now she knew Santi's old house and our house together. It gave me the heebie-jeebies.

The drive to Santi's house took about fifteen more minutes, and while I wanted to fill the disconcerting silence with words, I decided just to sit back. I'd bought myself another stop, and now I had to figure out what to do once we arrived.

When we parked in Santi's driveway, I wasn't sure if I was relieved that the new owners were really not there or disappointed, but I slowly walked around the front of the truck, as directed, and up to the front door, hoping this harebrained scheme I had concocted would work.

My keys were in my pants pocket, as they usually were, so I took them out and unlocked the front door. So far, Abigail didn't seem suspicious, so I tried to buy us more time. "She's been spending a lot of time in the back garden. I bet she's there now."

It was a lovely spring day, and if I had been able to, I would have been in a garden myself. Abigail seemed to be of the same mind and headed across the living room and kitchen to the back sliding glass door. I stayed close behind her, sure she'd react if I got too far away.

When she unlocked the back door, opened it, and stepped outside, I stopped walking and slammed the door shut, locking it behind her. She spun around and aimed the gun at me, but I sprinted to the front door, making it there just as I heard the glass break behind me.

I knew she would be after me in a minute, either by coming through the house or using the backyard gate, so I didn't hesitate. I ran with all my might toward town and headed straight for Mika's store. I didn't think Abigail could keep up with me, even though I was not a fast runner, even under the force of adrenaline. But then, she didn't have to catch me to be able to shoot me.

Fortunately, I turned onto Main Street and was inside Mika's shop with the door locked before Abigail rounded the corner. "Call Santi," I shouted as I ducked into the Cozy Nook and hid myself from view.

Mika didn't hesitate and picked up the phone, turning her body away from where I was hiding and just smiling at the older woman as Abigail reached the front window. Mika's casual attention apparently dissuaded Abigail from considering the yarn store as my location, so she kept walking.

"He'll be here in five minutes, and he said to let you know that Sawyer is okay."

A small whimper of relief came out of my mouth. But I stifled it when I heard the door shake and saw Mika post on a very fake smile. "She's back," Mika said without moving her lips. "Stay there," she said as she walked past me.

"Ma'am, I'm sorry. I've had a personal emer—"

The bell over the door rang violently, and I heard Mika say, "Excuse me."

The next thing I knew, Abigail grabbed me by the arm and dragged me toward the front door. "You almost made it, girly, but now, we're done." She opened the door and pushed me toward it.

I heard a sound behind me, and Abigail spun us both around. "You will stay here. And you will not say a word to anyone, or I will come back for you." The elderly woman could be very menacing when she wanted to.

"I've already called the police," Mika said. "They're on their way."

"Like I haven't heard that—" Abigail was face down on the ground before she could finish her sentence, and Forest was cuffing her.

"Are you okay?" Santi said as he stepped out from behind his deputy and pulled me against his chest.

I took a long, deep breath and let the scent of his cologne and his natural sage-like scent steady my nerves. "I'm okay," I said, stepping back. "I just probably need to see—"

A tiny body slammed into my legs. "Mom, we saved you." He sounded so grown up for a minute, but when I picked him up and pulled him to me, I saw just how scared my little boy had been. He started to shake and then cry, but society had already taught him tears were not acceptable for boys. So he wiped his eyes and pushed out of my arms in just a few seconds. Then he looked at Santi and stood in the exact same position, legs spread and arms crossed. It was adorable and heartbreaking.

"You did save me, Sawyer. Thank you."

"Yeah, bud," Santi added as he put a hand on Saw's shoulder. "That was smart thinking with your watch."

"Mom always said to call you if there was an emergency." He looked over at where Abigail now leaned against the wall. "Did you like how I talked in code?"

"Yeah, man, I did," Santi said. "Very smart."

"So that's how you got here so fast," Abigail said. "Smart kid," she repeated without joy. "I'm still due my treasure, you know?"

Santi looked at me. "Do you know what she's talking about?"

I shook my head. "Not a clue." Apparently, I was getting quite good at lying because I had a pretty big clue in mind.

Chapter Thirteen

After Forest had Abigail safely on her way to the cell at the sheriff's office, Mika brewed hot water and made tea for all of us. With his adrenaline spike clearly gone, Sawyer curled up in a chair and was asleep almost immediately. I could tell I wouldn't be far behind him, but first, I needed to give Santi my official statement and catch him up on my unofficial thought process.

My statement—the official one, at least—was delivered pretty quickly. I explained how Abigail had used Sawyer to lure me away and then ditched him, how I had convinced her Olivia was still alive, and how I'd run from her at Santi's old house. "We're going to owe them a new sliding glass door," I said.

"Maybe you can pay for it with Abigail's treasure?" Mika quipped.

Santi and I both shot her a look.

"Too soon?" she asked.

I rolled my eyes. "But speaking of treasure," I said. "We

need to talk about Dolores Cubbins." I filled them in on what Abigail had said. "I think it's still in the house."

Santi's eyes went wide. "In the secret room!"

Mika looked from him to me. "A secret room? What have I missed?"

As quickly as I could, I told Mika about the room Xzanthia and I had found, and then I turned to Santi and said, "Can we go now?"

"Yes, we can," he said. "Call Xzanthia, and I'll get Forest to join us. This is an all-hands-on-deck sort of situation."

I was surprised he wanted all of us there, but then, Xzanthia and I were the ones who knew how to get in the room. And I suspected he felt bad leaving Mika out after the scare earlier.

He was on his phone as we walked to his cruiser, parked half on the curb outside. I got in the front, and Mika climbed in the back with Sawyer, who didn't even wake up when she strapped him in the car seat, and within a minute, we were heading up the road to the McNamara house.

When we pulled up, the house was dark, and since it was almost sunset, we couldn't see much in the yard. But it didn't look like anyone was there. So we made our way onto the porch, used the code to open the lockbox, and let ourselves in.

"Isn't this trespassing?" Mika asked.

"We have probable cause," Santi said, "so no." He sounded sure of himself, so I went with it, even though I wasn't so sure myself.

Forest pulled up and stationed himself on the front porch, and Xzanthia joined us a moment later. My heart was racing again as I led the way in the door with my phone's flashlight shining into the darkening room.

On the floor inside sat Peter Cubbins. He looked up when we came in but didn't look surprised.

"Mr. Cubbins, why are you here?" Santi asked as he gave the man his hand and pulled him to his feet.

"The same reason you are, I imagine." He pointed to the corner where the secret room was supposedly located. "Dolores has gone, and she left me a note about the treasure not being worth it anymore. She said she was sorry, but if I found it, she might come back."

I sighed. "Do you even know what we're looking for?" He seemed so distraught, yet he had been here—same as everyone apparently—trying to find the treasure before anyone else. I was kind of sick of human beings.

"I don't," he said, "and I know it may not seem like it, but I was actually hoping to figure this out and tell you, Sheriff. I knew she'd been hiding something because she'd been so adamant about buying this house and then destroying it." He shook his head. "It just didn't make sense."

"Well, please step back, Mr. Cubbins. Whatever we find here will become evidence in two murder investigations. So it won't be going anywhere but with me for the time being." Santi had assumed his sheriff's voice now, and he meant business.

"Yes, of course," Cubbins said, stepping back toward the door.

"Xzanthia, would you do the honors?" Santi asked.

My friend stepped forward, placed her large but graceful hands on the pillar in front of her, and twisted in clockwise. Just as in Caroline and Thad's house, a small click sounded, and a door opened just where we expected it to.

What we didn't expect to find was a room full of costume jewelry, hundreds and thousands of pieces, all displayed carefully on shelves or corkboards. It was a glittering gallery that flashed against our flashlights.

"Wow," I said as I stepped in and spun around. All four walls were covered from floor to ceiling. "If these pieces are worth anything like the Christmas tree. . ." I couldn't even finish my sentence.

Santi whistled. "It does resemble treasure, I have to say."

"It does," Xzanthia said. "But no treasure is worth a life."

"Let alone two," I said. "Abigail Toperman. . ." I let my voice trail off because I didn't know what to say about a woman who would kill two people for some jewelry.

"Why do you think Viola McNamara left it here?" Xzanthia asked. "Why didn't she take this with her when she moved out?"

"Beats me, but if she had, we might have avoided this whole mess," I said.

It took a few days for all the details to get sorted out about what exactly happened to Viola McNamara, why she had left her "treasure" in the house, and what would happen to it now. But by the weekend, Santi had put together a lot more of the story.

It turned out that Lucy, Abigail, and Viola had worked together to amass the small fortune—almost $400,000 at the low end of the estimate—of costume jewelry by visiting rummage sales, thrift stores, auctions, and flea markets. It had been their weekend hobby for years, a way for them to have some spending cash in their retirement.

But, according to Lucy, Viola had paid for everything. When it came time for them to divide up the spoils, Viola had refused, telling her friends that she wanted to leave the collection to Olivia and had been unwilling to tell them where she kept it.

"And that's why she didn't want to move it when she left the house," Mika said when Santi told us the latest over Friday night pizza at our house. "They were there, and she didn't want them to know."

"Precisely," Santi said.

"And they didn't know about the secret room at all?" Xzanthia said as she cut another bite-size piece from her slice of pepperoni.

"Nope," Santi said as he poured us all some more iced tea. "But the two women suspected it was in the house. So when Abigail saw Viola returning to her old home, she confronted her about her portion of the treasure."

"And when Viola still refused, she killed her." I sighed. "With what?"

"A cast-iron skillet," Santi said. "She actually seemed kind of proud of that."

I shuddered as I remembered the collection of cast-iron cookware at Abigail's house. "That's just horrible."

Santi nodded. "It is. Not saying what Viola did was right, but she didn't deserve to die for it." He took a big bite of his Hawaiian slice and chewed thoughtfully.

"What did Lucy Somerall have to say about all this?" Xzanthia asked.

"That's pretty interesting, actually," Santi continued after he swallowed. "She felt caught between her two friends. She didn't care much about the jewelry, but she did care about Viola and Abigail. And when the two were fighting, all she wanted was peace."

"I guess she'll get that now," Mika said. "But maybe in the most horrible way possible."

I nodded. "How did Dolores Cubbins get involved?"

Santi grinned. "Turns out she saw the blueprints at the historical society and made the same judgment you did about the secret room but couldn't figure out how to open it."

Xzanthia shook her head. "And here I thought she was just interested in the history of her new home." She sighed. "That's too bad. I might have been able to help if she had just asked."

"Greed can make fools of us all," Mary said as she helped herself to more pizza. "What will happen to the jewelry?"

"Well, Viola McNamara has no living heirs or family, so all her remaining estate goes to a charity over in Orange, the Tuskin Club." Santi smiled at me.

"She left everything to a cause her true love adored," I said as tears pooled in my eyes. "That's so sweet. Does he know?"

"I told him this morning, and he's thrilled. And sad." Santi rubbed his hands over his face. "It's a tragedy in so many ways."

I leaned my head against his shoulder. "It is. It really, really is."

"At least," Mary said, "they both lived good lives— maybe lonely lives, but good ones."

We let a small silence fill the room as the truth of Mary's words sunk in.

Then, Mika stood up and said, "But you know what's not a tragedy, this chocolate cake I made with Mary's help. Who wants a slice?"

Every hand in our small kitchen went up. Sometimes, love looked like sweet tea and chocolate cake on a warm spring evening in a farmhouse kitchen.

Also by ACF Bookens

vinci-books.com/BastedButchery

In Paisley's world, every stitch tells a story—and some end in murder.

When a body surfaces at the historic Brown Plantation, Paisley Sutton's quiet weekend turns into a hunt for a killer. As she pieces together secrets stitched into the past, she learns some histories refuse to stay buried.

Turn the page for a free preview…

Basted Butchery: Chapter One

I don't really know what I was thinking when I picked up this cross-stitch kit. I'd been nannying for a friend in Baltimore, and I realized, as I always do when I think I'm going to be all "see the town" in a new place, that all I wanted to do was relax, sew, and watch their limitless supply of TV channels. Their child had been a delight all day, but I was tired. I need something soothing to do, so I ran out to the nearest craft store and bought the funnest kit I could find, thinking I'd make it for my mom.

And that is how, more than a decade later, I was now untangling strands of embroidery floss, trying to figure out how to read the pattern, and deciding if I really wanted to go back in to stitch Maggie, the cat who had made herself at home in the pattern's sewing room. Santiago had taken Sawyer fishing for a week up in West Virginia, and I had a massive salvage job starting on Monday at the farm next door. So this weekend, I was going to sit, stitch, and catch up on all the shows that I couldn't watch while Sawyer was in the house. He thought he was old enough to swear like a sailor, but I still held that age 6 was a bit young for such language. Whew!

After spending the first episode of *High Potential* detangling, I decided I was going to finish the kit. For anyone who knew me, this decision would have come as no surprise because I was a finisher, to a fault. If I hated a meal I'd ordered, rather than ask for something else, I just ate it. A book bored me to tears through three chapters, it didn't matter; I was finishing that sucker. And thus, I had an entire antique hatbox full of half-done projects like this one. I'd just turned 50, and it was time for me to wrap up some stuff or send it on. Since the very idea of sending it on made my heart race, finishing up it was.

In reality, the project didn't matter that much to me as long as I had something to stitch on this quiet, solitary weekend. Sometimes, just the idea of stitching relaxed me, the colors, the patterns, the simplicity of the stitch itself...I could think about it and calm down almost instantly.

This afternoon, though, I was especially excited to get to it because it was still daylight, which meant the stitching was easier on my eyes and because I had hours before my late bedtime of 10pm. There was only so much I was willing to screw up my sleep schedule even when I was going to have a week alone. That 6:30am wake-up on Sawyer's first day back at school was going to be hard enough as it was.

For three hours, I lost myself in ridiculous police drama and stitches, and when I finally gave in to my hunger around 6, I found I was absolutely famished and really had to pee. I had realized that I often did this to myself when I was alone – I just put off my body's needs until they were urgent, not so much out of self-neglect as out of lack of awareness. It had been that way my whole life, in fact. In school, I'd wait to go to the bathroom until I was at home, and it was a close call sometimes, because I was too over-whelmed by everything there to even think about going to the bathroom.

Now, I realized that was part of my ADHD, a diagnosis I'd only gotten in the last year, and while the diagnosis helped me understand why I did that, I hadn't yet landed on the thing that would help me overcome this tendency. I was just counting it a win that I had set a timer on my phone to remind me to drink something every two hours. Clearly, that was why I now had to pee.

I was just coming out of the bathroom with a plan to make myself grilled cheese and tomato soup for dinner when I saw a light across the stream. The farm across the way had been empty for as long as I'd lived here, and while it had been recently sold to a family who wanted to restore it – the family for whom I'd be working next week in fact – it seemed odd that someone would be poking around with what looked like a flashlight at dusk on a Friday evening.

Normally, I would have just let Santi know, but since he was in another state, I decided to just take a ride over there and check it out myself. Of course, I let my best friend Mika know what I was doing, but when I heard her reply come almost immediately, I ignored it. She wasn't going to like that I was going. I, however, was giving myself credit for being responsible enough to tell someone. I hadn't always done that. *Take your win where you can get it, Miks,* I thought.

While the distance to the Brown Plantation over the stream was quite short as the crow flies, the actual road wound around through what used to be a town, over a one-lane bridge, and then up a roadside to a long, gravel drive-way. Walking, I could have been there in 5 minutes. Driving, it took me 7.

When I pulled up to the brick Federal-style house, I felt

a little thrill. The building hadn't been altered much in the last two hundred years since it had been built, and because the enslaved people who built it were clearly skilled crafts-men, the structure was still quite solid and beautiful. I knew the inside had seen better days – the new owners had emailed me some pictures – but the main house and the outbuildings were still very solid.

Not seeing any lights around the big house, I wandered around to the north side, where most of the outbuildings stood. The dairy was still there as were the stables, a black-smith's shed, and the building I was most excited about – the old weavers' shed In the days when the plantation had been built, the women who wove the clothing for everyone on the farm had worked in here, and from the pictures, I knew that two huge spinning wheels were still intact inside. But as excited as I was, I wasn't dumb enough to go poking around in dead buildings alone at dusk. While it wasn't likely we'd have snakes this time of year, we did have black widows and worn-out floorboards. I wasn't keen to spend the night with my leg dangling through a hole while a red-bellied spider decided if I was a threat.

So I just wandered slowly around the buildings. My eyes were pretty accustomed to the dark in the country, some-thing that amazed all my friends who lived in cities, so I didn't turn on the flashlight on my phone. The gloaming gave me plenty of light to see, and my circuit around the buildings didn't reveal anyone. I had just decided maybe it was someone talking a stroll or looking for a lost dog when I caught a flash of light from the corner of my eye. It was heading into the woods behind the outbuildings, up and away from the stream.

I was reckless, but I wasn't that reckless. So I just waited to be sure they didn't come back, and then I started back toward my car, looking up the new owner's number as I went. I stood by my car, debating whether or not to tell them what had just happened. I decided against it, though, since it didn't seem like anything had been disturbed. No need to worry them unnecessarily. Then, just as I was opening my car door, I heard the sound of a loud truck engine off in the direction that the light had gone.

It used to be that I knew nothing about trucks, but since I'd married a man whose one country streak related to pick-ups, I'd learned a lot. I could tell from the sound of the engine that the muffler had been straightened to make it louder, and when it turned onto the paved road, I heard the wheeze of the mud tires. That wasn't enough to differentiate it from all the other loud pick-ups with mud tires, but it was something.

For now, though, I needed food, a glass of wine, and more TV and sewing. As soon as I turned down my driveway, though, I saw Mika's little sedan in the driveway, and then, I noticed that she was sitting on my porch, a quilt wrapped around her, and her phone in her hand. As soon as I opened the car door, she said, "I was giving it two more minutes, and then I was calling the police."

I rolled my eyes. "I'm fine. No problems," I said. "I just didn't want to take any risks by going out without letting someone know where I was." I started to walk past her and invite her into the house where I had, of all things, heat, but her open-mouthed stared caught my attention even in the periphery. "What?"

"You seriously think that going to an abandoned farm after dark alone isn't risky?" She stared at me harder.

"Well, no, but at least I texted you, right?"

"Right. So I could worry without the ability to do

anything about it except to do what might have been considered overreacting. That's a great choice."

She was really mad, and while I didn't fully understand why, I definitely hadn't intended to worry her. I turned and put my hands on her arms. "I'm sorry, Miks. I didn't mean to worry you." I held her gaze until she let out a long sigh, and I knew that she was okay. "I'm really sorry."

She wrapped her arm around my waist. "Thank you for apologizing. Can we go in now? I need to sit by your fire."

"Of course," I said. "Did you bring a project? Because I have soup, grilled cheese, and some more TV to watch."

She pointed to a tote bag next to my kitchen peninsula. "Of course, and tomato soup?"

"You know it," I said. The two of us fell into an easy rhythm, making my comfort dinner just the way my mom had made it – sliced grocery store, whole wheat bread, thick slices of sharp cheddar, lots of butter, and tomato soup made with the requested one can of water. No special herbs. No cream. No fancy spread on the bread. Just basic as the days when she made it for me after snowball fights. Mika knew the drill, and soon, we were settled back in with our food on the ottoman, our handwork at our side, and our eyes glued to the television.

Normally, I might have resented someone interrupting my weekend of solitude, but having Mika with me was like being with myself but funnier. I had someone to snark with, and she alternated trips to the kitchen with me when we needed more wine or snacks. But she didn't require me to be anyone but myself. This is why she was my best friend.

We stayed up way too late one-more-episode-ing ourselves, but eventually, she climbed into Sawyer's bed and I into mine, and when I finally dragged myself from bed the next morning, she was gone, a note on the table that said,

"Don't sew too hard." It was a sort of private joke with us because we'd both given ourselves repetitive use injuries from our sewing and crocheting. She was teasing, but she also wasn't. Neither of us wanted to have hand surgery.

So rather than just immediately sitting back down, turning on my audio book, and starting to stitch again, I puttered about the house a bit, doing the kind of things I usually just ignored because I didn't have the time, focus, or energy. So by the time I returned to my slightly concave cushion on the couch, the cabinet doors were gleaming, Beauregard's litter box was deep-cleaned, and the laundry was actually already in the dryer.

If Beau, the Maine Coon, had been a dog, I would have considered that his desire to snuggle up close and go to sleep as soon as I sat down was gratitude for his clean bathroom, but I knew better. He was cold. I was warm-blooded. He would tolerate me so that he could siphon away my heat, just as he tolerated the walk to the car in the winter because he could take full advantage of the heated seat as I chauffeured him around his fiefdom.

Still, I welcomed the quiet rumble of his begrudging purr and did, indeed, stitch the day away. But as dusk began to settle, I found myself at the front windows of my house watching the Brown Plantation to see if I saw lights there again. I didn't, and most of me was relieved …except for that little part that was just so curious about what someone had been doing over there the night before.

Fortunately, I saw that a new episode of *Rescue: High Surf* had become available on streaming, and I was distracted enough by that prospect to put away the twinge of a thought that might have sent me back there to poke around again. These kinds of urges never hit me in daylight, when my brain was fully functional and the tiredness of a day of doing almost nothing hadn't zapped me. And I reminded myself that if I went, tomorrow not only would Mika and Santi be mortified, I would probably feel a bit chagrined myself.

Instead, I forced myself to watch beautiful people in a beautiful place saving lives and creating drama in their own. Then, I picked up the grumpy cat and went to bed.

Sunday rolled by in much the same way as Saturday, except perhaps less productively. Aside from the enjoyment and nostalgia I got attending services with my friend Mary from time to time, I wasn't much of a church goer anymore. As I told most people, God and I were good, but the church and I had some stuff to work out. Still, though, that Sabbath day was built into my life's rhythm, so I was able to let myself fully relax on Sundays without guilt even. So I took full advantage and just lazed and napped and stitched all day, living off granola bars and my water bottle. It was simple but luxurious.

Plus, the effects of all that rest and relaxation were that when Monday morning rolled around, I was genuinely energized and excited to get to work over at the Brown Place, and not just because I was curious to see if I could figure out why someone had been poking around in the dark. I was scheduled to meet the new owners over there at 9am, so about 8:30, when I had resisted the urge to go over for a full hour and had chosen to fold my laundry instead, I got my new high-resolution camera (a Christmas present from my husband), my notebook, and my pen and headed over, walking this time.

When I made it up the hill by the big house just before 9, I was slightly sweaty but even more energetic, my blood really pumping from the steep hike up the hill from the stream. Fortunately, though, I was the first one there, so I had a few minutes to catch my breath. Nothing like huffing and puffing through your first in-person meeting with your new clients.

While I let my heart rate settle, I strolled around the property, this time peeking in windows and open outbuilding doors rather than both hoping and not hoping that I would find someone else there. Instead, I was mentally cataloging possible items to salvage – windows and floorboards, mostly, but I also saw a great mantel in one room, and I wasn't sure, but I thought there might have still been an anvil in the blacksmith's shop.

The new owners, the Abramses, were a couple from DC. The plantation was going to be their vacation home but also a place where they focused the storytelling around the people who had been enslaved there. The aim was to have a high-end hotel that was available at a more moderate price than many of the fine hotels in the area and that was intended to draw African American visitors. Thus, they were renovating all the outbuildings to be guest suites, but they were also going to keep them thematically connected to their original purposes.

So unlike the buildings that I usually salvaged from, where things were going to be gutted or demolished, the Abramses wanted to save as much as they could while also being reasonable about what was needed to make the space a luxury hotel. That's why we were meeting today – they wanted to inventory what I would take and what, in my opinion, could be saved and used with a little polish. So we were planning a day of inspecting everything to help with my salvage plans and their remodeling ones.

I was just walking up onto the front porch of the main house when I heard tires crunching behind me. There, in their beautiful maroon Cadillac, were Willie and William

Abrams. They had immediately joked about their names when we first talked, and their ability to see the humor in themselves had won me over immediately. Willie was a small woman with long braids, skinny jeans, and the best bejeweled eyeglasses I'd ever seen. William was tall and broad-shouldered, built like a lineman, which made sense since he had played professional football in his not-so-distant past. I waved enthusiastically as they walked toward the house, and when Willie stepped up next to me and gave me a hug, I immediately liked her, and not just because she smelled like coconut and fresh air. She actually hugged me, tight. I loved a person who gave me a real hug.

William stooped slightly and put out his oven mitt of a hand for me to shake. My fingers barely encircled his, but his smile took away any intimidation I might have felt at his size. "Paisley, it's so nice to meet you," he said in a resonant voice. "Thank you for meeting us here. I hope you didn't have to come far."

I laughed and pointed behind me. "I can see your new place from mine. I'm in the little blue house across the bridge."

"What?!" Willie said. "We're going to be neighbors. See, another sign that we are on the right path." She looked at her husband and winked.

"Never doubted it," he said. "So where do we start, Ms. Salvage?"

I chuckled and thought, for a second, about what that name might look like on a T-shirt. But I forced myself to focus and said, "If it's okay with you, let's start in the main house. Since you'll be living there, I imagine you're going to want to get it livable first."

"Actually," Willie said, "We're going to live in the old weavers' shed, leave the big house for guests."

"Oh," I said, my affection for these people growing by the minute. "I love that. Do you want to start there, instead?"

"Yes, let's," William said. "We're not going to do anything fancy in there. Just a comfortable bedroom and bath."

"You know, I think that's so wise. I really value my alone time, and this way you guys will have yours," I said as we walked to the shed.

"That's exactly what we were thinking. We'll mingle with our guests at meals and in the kitchen, but it'll also be nice to have our own place to relax and get a break," Willie said as she pushed open the unlatched door on the shed. "That's odd," she said as she flipped the open padlock on the door. "I thought we'd locked this up."

"We were in and out so fast last time ...we probably just forgot," William said.

Once again, I debated on whether or not to say anything about the visitor from Friday. I decided, though, that it was best to be forthright, so I quickly mentioned that I'd seen a light up here, that I'd come to check it out, and that I'd seen the person leave without, as far as I could tell, disturbing anything.

William frowned at me. "You came up here by yourself?"

"He was here by the shed when I arrived." I didn't say anymore, but my implication was clear.

William bent down to look at the dangling lock. "It doesn't look like it's been broken or jimmied." He dropped the lock. "We're the only ones with a key, so we must have just forgotten." He looked at his wife and smiled. "It's okay."

She didn't look convinced, and I certainly had a lot of

questions that led me to my own doubts. Had they put the lock on the door, or had it already been there? Could anyone else – like the realtor or a handyman – have a copy of the key? Was this one of those locks that could be picked with a ballpoint pen? I didn't say anything, though. Everything did look fine, and withal the trouble of the world, why borrow more?

The door opened smoothly, and inside, I was delighted to see that the floors were in good shape. "These can just be cleaned and kept, in my opinion." The boards were wide and rough and old. Heart pine, it looked like. "If you don't mind a little more rough texture."

"They are gorgeous," Willie said, bending down and running her fingers over the boards. "Yes, we'll keep those."

"The windows are in great shape, and they have original glass. But they'll not be terribly efficient or warm. That's your call," I continued as I moved around the roughly fifteen foot by fifteen foot space.

The couple looked to one another, and I took a few steps away to give them the privacy I could in the small room. The back wall featured a fireplace made from hand-shaped bricks, and a small beam served as a rough mantel.

"If you'll take the windows, Paisley," Willie said, "we'll replace them with more efficient ones."

I made a note and then pointed at the fireplace. "You'll want to have this evaluated if you want to use it. I expect that at the least you'll need to have it repointed, but it might also need a sleeve."

"We won't use it," William said. "Can you salvage the bricks and the mantel?"

"I can," I said, secretly delighted and peered behind the bricks. "It looks like the wall is in pretty good shape behind it, but of course there will be some repair work that needs to be done."

"We've already contracted with Saul to do the repair work," William said. "Based on your fine recommendation."

Saul was Mika's biological uncle and my adopted one. He was an expert historical contractor and also the landlord for my architectural salvage shop that sat on his construction lot. He was one of my favorite people in the world, and I was glad to hear the Abramses had hired him.

"Excellent," I said. "He'll know just what to do here." I made another note and then, finally, addressed the items that had caught my eye as soon as we walked in – long bolts of vintage fabrics all stacked in the corner of the room and two spinning wheels. "How about this fabric?" I said.

"It's beautiful," Willie said as she fingered what looked to be a paisley pattern on a dupioni silk. "But we don't have any need of it, right?" She looked to her husband.

"Nope," he agreed.

"Not even for curtains or such?" I could feel my excitement building, but before I got my hopes up about the delight these bolts of fabric would elicit in my customer base, I wanted to be sure the Abramses were sure.

"Nope, we're going with a more modern palette," Willie said and then laughed. "I sound so pretentious."

"Next time I come over, I'll expect you to be wearing white gloves and smoking a cigarette in a holder," I joked.

"Better that than some plantation hoop skirt or some such," William said with a chuckle.

"Very true," I said. "Okay, I'll take these with me today, probably. Just to clear the space for the rest of the retrieval." I looked up at the ceiling, which was exposed beams and the roof boards under the metal sheeting above. "If I were you, I'd just clean that up and leave it. It's beautiful." I smiled at my new clients. "But of course, if you need me to help with anything else in here, let me know."

"And you'll take the spinning wheels, of course," Willie said.

I grinned. "I'd love to, again, if you don't want them for décor," I said.

"We're not using anything more about the enslaved people's labor than is necessary for the running of the hotel. We're reclaiming this space as our own," William said. "So no, as beautiful and important as they are, we will not be using them."

"Understood," I said and made a mental note to consider how I might repurpose one of these to reclaim it the same way.

We moved on to the wagon shed, which included several wagon wheels and an old Coca-Cola chest cooler. William claimed the cooler for the bar space he was creating in the basement of the house, but the wheels were all mine. Most of the other outbuildings were full of old furniture, all of which I offered to take and dispose of if it wasn't salvageable. The Abramses agreed, and we entered the main house to do our final round of scouting. Here, the couple wanted to keep most of the finer elements – the mantels, the wainscoting, the chair rails and crown moulding. They didn't say as much, but I gathered they wanted to have these adornments for the same reason they didn't want to have the reminders of labor – the people who had created them, the talented craftspeople that they were, were not allowed to enjoy the fruits of their own fine labor. Now, though, maybe some of their descendants would, and if not their direct kin, at least those people who inherited freedom from their perseverance and determination.

I did make note of the windows in the house since they

were going to be replaced with exact replicas that were much more efficient. And there was a classic set of sunshine yellow kitchen appliances that, as best I could tell, were all in working order that the Abramses were delighted to hear I'd rid them of.

My plan was to come back with Saul and his crew the next day to load a truck with most of the items, but today, I wanted to get a look at that fabric and put it up on my site. My Subaru was just big enough to fit all the rolls, so I headed back to the weavers' House with William to get them out of the building. It took us a couple of trips, but we managed to get the first eight rolls into the station wagon without any trouble. I was headed back from the car to get some of the final few rolls when I heard William shout for help.

I sprinted the rest of the way to the shed, but I came to a fast stop when I saw that William was holding a roll of plastic with a human head sticking out.

"Call the police," he said.

Basted Butchery: Chapter Two

Of course, my first instinct was to text Santi. He was always faster to respond than 911, even though both his officers and the EMTs were excellent, but I had given my son my word that I wouldn't interrupt their week. Sawyer was very excited to spend the week with his stepdad, and I knew that if he got wind of this situation, he would be home within hours. I wouldn't do that to Sawyer, not when Santi's staff was quite capable of handling the situation.

So like any normal Octonia citizen, I called 911, told the dispatcher that we'd found a body at the old Brown place, and asked her to send officers and am ambulance. I couldn't imagine that anyone who had been wrapped in plastic was still alive, but I also wasn't willing to take a chance on that.

Then, I slipped my phone into my pocket and helped William lay the body down flat on the floor of the shed. The person was slight, but a human body was heavy, especially when said human couldn't help move their own body.

"Now, we need to leave him be," I said to William. He had started to unwrap the plastic but stopped immediately. "The police will need to see him as he is."

William took a few steps back. "Right. Right," he said. "So you think he's a man, too."

"I do," I said, "but of course, he'll need to be identified for us to be sure of his gender."

"Right, right," William said again. "Of course."

I didn't think my client was actually processing much of anything at the moment, and I couldn't blame him. Unfortunately, I'd found more than my fair share of dead bodies, and while I would definitely have to take some time and process this experience later, I was past the initial shock. "Why don't we go sit on the porch? Let Willie know what happened."

I put my hand on the small of the giant man's back and steered him to the porch, where I pointed at the rocking chair and told him to sit. Then, I went in and found Willie, where she was unpacking dishes into the kitchen cabinets. "Can you come to the porch?" I said.

She put down the stack of simple, white plates and followed me out the door. "What's wrong?" she asked as she saw her husband sitting with his head in his hands.

I quickly told her that we had found a body in the weavers' shed and that the police were on the way. "I didn't know him," I said and only then realized what a strange thing that was to say. Of course I didn't know him.

Willie nodded at me. "Okay, Okay." She put her hand on William's back and began making small circles, like the ones my mom used to make on my back to comfort me, like the ones I made on Sawyer's now. Just the sight of the gestured calmed me a bit.

Moments later, I heard tires on the gravel drive and went out to meet Alan Forest, my husband's deputy. The man had become a good friend to us in the few months since he'd started working at the Octonia Sheriff's Office, and he was a good police officer. So while he smiled at me when I greeted him, he was all business and went immediately to the Abramses. "Ma'am, sir," he said. "I'm Deputy Forest. Can you tell me what you found?"

William looked up at me, and I gave him a nod. I was there, too, but this was his property. It was better he take the lead on the situation rather than deferring to me, even if I was the sheriff's wife. "There's a body," he said. "Over there." He pointed toward the weavers' shed. "It's wrapped in plastic. Was hidden behind some bolts of fabric."

"Some of those bolts are in my car because they were salvaged, but I'll get them back out if need be," I added.

"Did you recognize him?" Forest said after a curt nod to acknowledge my statement.

William shook his head and so did I. "Never seen him before," I said and noted Forest's quick note.

"Anything else you noticed that I should know about?" the deputy asked.

Willie and William looked at me, and I took a deep breath. "Yes, on Friday night, I saw someone snooping around the property."

Forest's eyebrows furrowed. "I need the details please. Were you here?"

I nodded and then quickly recounted what I had seen both from home and from up here at the Abrams's place. I even went so far as to describe the sound of the truck and its tires. "You know those mud tires, the ones that sound like a rocket launching when they get going?" I finished.

A small smile played at the corner of Forest's mouth. "Yes, I know what mud tires sound like, Paisley." He glanced up from his notebook. "I'm actually kind of impressed you do, though."

I sighed. "Grow up in the country and date enough country boys, you begin to innately know all kinds of things that you wished you could use that brain space for."

"Well, in this case, your ear for tire sounds might just come in handy." He looked at each of us as he said, "Anything else?"

We all shook our heads, and he slipped the notebook and pen back into his pocket. "Alright then. I need to look around. If you'll just point me to the body. . ."

William led him over to the weavers' shed and then waited outside while the deputy examined the body. "I'll need to call the coroner and get crime scene techs out here, but it looks like he was strangled …and some time ago."

As the deputy took his phone out of his pocket, I asked, "What do you mean 'some time ago?'"

"Can't be sure until we get word from the coroner, but I think our victim was embalmed."

The shiver that ran through my body made my teeth clack together.

"What do you mean he was embalmed? Like a mummy?" Willie's eyes were wide, and there was a quaver in her voice.

"Like I said, I'm not sure, but I thought I smelled formaldehyde." He looked at me and gave a subtle shake of his head.

"Let's not think about that," I said. "Willie, do you have some tea in there? Maybe with a shot of whiskey?"

My question seemed to jerk her thoughts away from the

body, and she, as most Southern woman are inclined to do by training if not by choice, turned into a hostess on the spot. "Yes, I do. Deputy, may I bring you some tea?"

"Yes, ma'am," Forest said with an actual tip of his ball cap. "No whiskey for me, though, being as I'm on duty and all."

She gave him a small smile, and when William looked at me, I tilted my head as a suggestion that he follow.

"Now, what are you saying, Deputy?" I whispered as soon as the couple was out of ear shot.

He leaned toward me. "You've seen enough dead bodies to know what they look like just after death, right?"

I shuddered but nodded my head. Unfortunately, I did know.

"Well, this one doesn't look, er, fresh," he said with a wince. "Maybe I'm wrong. Tell me if I am."

I followed him back to the weavers' shed, and for the first time, I looked down at the victim. Forest wasn't wrong. This man had been dead for a while, but he didn't look like he was decaying. Maybe *mummifying* was the better word. "I see what you mean," I said and stepped back out of the shed. I didn't need even more images of dead people clouding my mind on the daily, but it was curious, disturbing, too, that this person had been dead for a while and was just in the shed.

A thought occurred to me. "Do you think whoever was here on Friday night might have put the body there then? Or do you think it's been here since, well, since it was prepared?"

Forest shook his head. "I don't know, Pais. But it's definitely odd. I could hazard a lot of theories right now, but I'm going with Santi's way on this one."

"Follow the evidence," I said in a slightly deeper voice that I lilted to mimic the slight hint of a Mexican accent that he had inherited from his mother.

Forest smiled. "Exactly."

Grab your copy…
vinci-books.com/BastedButchery

About the Author

ACF Bookens lives at the edge of Virginia's Blue Ridge Mountains with her young son and three playful cats. When she's not writing, she cross-stitches, plays too much Roblox with her kid, and does historical research on enslaved communities in the area.

www.ingramcontent.com/pod-product-compliance
Lightning Source LLC
Chambersburg PA
CBHW011749010726
47498CB00012B/2983